Presenting a

from

A Se

A lad ***...tells...***

Elena Leighton and Ellie Rosewood might only be a lowly governess and a lady's companion, but there is more to these women than meets the eye!

For their meek and respectable demeanor hides this season's most scandalous secrets... and all is about to be deliciously revealed!

How far will the Duke of Royston go to lay bare the real Ellie Rosewood?
NOT JUST A WALLFLOWER
December 2013

And Lord Adam Hawthorne makes a date with impropriety in
NOT JUST A GOVERNESS
Already available

and in ebooks from Harlequin Historical *Undone!*
NOT JUST A SEDUCTION
Already available

Carole Mortimer

Not Just a Wallflower

Available from Harlequin® Historical and CAROLE MORTIMER

**The Duke's Cinderella Bride* #960
**The Rake's Wicked Proposal* #969
**The Rogue's Disgraced Lady* #975
**Lady Arabella's Scandalous Marriage* #987
Regency Christmas Proposals #1015
*"Christmas at Mulberry Hall"
Δ*The Lady Gambles* #1066
Δ*The Lady Forfeits* #1070
Δ*The Lady Confesses* #1072
****Some Like It Wicked* #1116
****Some Like to Shock* #1120
§*Not Just a Governess* #1148
§*Not Just a Wallflower* #1164

Other works include

HQN

¤*The Wicked Lord Montague*

Harlequin Historical *Undone!* ebooks

**At the Duke's Service*
Convenient Wife, Pleasured Lady
Δ*A Wickedly Pleasurable Wager*
****Some Like It Scandalous*
§*Not Just a Seduction*

*The Notorious St. Claires
ΔThe Copeland Sisters
**Daring Duchesses
§A Season of Secrets
¤part of Castonbury Park Regency miniseries

Did you know that these novels are also available as ebooks? Visit www.Harlequin.com.

Carole Mortimer also writes for Harlequin Presents!

Chapter One

June, 1817—Lady Cicely Hawthorne's London home

'You must be absolutely thrilled at the news of Hawthorne's forthcoming marriage to Miss Matthews!' Lady Jocelyn Ambrose, Dowager Countess of Chambourne, beamed across the tea table at her hostess.

Lady Cicely nodded. 'The match was not without its...complications, but I have no doubts that Adam and Magdelena will deal very well together.'

The dowager countess sobered. 'How is she now that all the unpleasantness has been settled?'

'Very well.' Lady Cicely smiled warmly. 'She is, I am happy to report, a young lady of great inner strength.'

'She had need of it when that rogue Sheffield was doing all that he could to ruin her, socially as well as financially.' Edith St Just, Dowager Duchess of Royston, and the third in the trio of friends, said, sniffing disdainfully.

Edith gave a satisfied smile. 'By which time St Just will, I assure you, find himself well and truly leg-shackled!'

'You are still convinced it will be to the lady whom you have named in the note held by my own butler?' Lady Jocelyn also looked less than confident about the outcome of this enterprise.

At the same time as the three ladies had laid their plans to ensure their grandsons found their brides that Season, the dowager duchess had also announced she had already made her choice of bride for her own grandson, and that Royston would find himself betrothed to that lady by the end of the Season. So confident had she been of her choice that she had accepted the other ladies' dare to write down the name of that young lady and leave it in the safe keeping of Edwards, Lady Jocelyn's butler, to be opened and verified on the day Royston announced his intention of marrying.

'I am utterly convinced,' Edith now stated confidently.

'But, to my knowledge, Royston has not expressed a preference for any of the young ladies of the current Season.' Lady Cicely, the most tender-hearted of the three, could not bear the thought of her dear friend being proved wrong.

'Nor will he,' the dowager duchess revealed mysteriously.

'But—'

'We must not press dear Edith any further.' Lady Jocelyn reached across to gently squeeze Lady Cice-

Chapter Two

Two days later—White's Club, St James's Street, London

'Is it not time you threw in your cards and called it a night, Litchfield?'

'You'd like it if I did so, wouldn't you, Royston!' The florid, sneering face of the man seated on the opposite side of the card table was slightly damp with perspiration in the dimmed candlelight of the smoky card room.

'I have no opinion one way or the other if you should decide to lose the very shirt upon your back,' Justin St Just, the Duke of Royston, drawled as he reclined back in his armchair, only the glittering intensity of his narrowed blue eyes revealing the utter contempt he felt for the other man. 'I merely wish to bring this interminable game of cards to an end!' He deeply regretted having accepted Litchfield's challenge now, and knew he would not have done so if he had not been utterly bored and seeking any diversion to relieve him from it.

fashionably overlong golden hair, and arrogantly handsome features, he resembled a fallen angel far more than he did the devil. But regardless of how angelic he looked, most, if not all, of the gentlemen of the *ton* also knew him to be an expert with both the usual choices of weapon for the duel Litchfield was spoiling for. 'As I have said, the sooner we bring this card game to an end, the better.'

'You arrogant bastard!' Litchfield glared across at him fiercely; he was a man perhaps a dozen or so years older than Justin's own eight and twenty, but his excessive weight, thinning auburn hair liberally streaked with silver, brown-stained teeth from an over-indulgence in cheap cigars, as well as his blustering anger at his consistent bad luck with the cards, all resulted in him looking much older.

'I do not believe insulting me will succeed in improving your appalling skill at the cards,' Justin stated as he replaced his brandy glass on the table.

'You—'

'Excuse me, your Grace, but this was just delivered for your immediate attention.'

A silver tray appeared out of the surrounding smoke-hazed gloom, bearing a note with Justin's name scrawled across the front of it, written in a hand that a single glance had shown was not familiar to him. 'If you will excuse me, Litchfield?' He did not so much as glance in the other man's direction as he retrieved the note from the tray to break the seal and quickly read the contents before refolding it and placing it in the pocket

last contemptuous glance, he wasted no more time as he turned to stride purposefully from the dimly lit room, nodding briefly to several acquaintances as he did so.

'Step aside, Royston!'

Justin's legendary reflexes allowed him to take that swift sideways step and turn all at the same time, eyes widening as he watched a fist making contact with the lunging and livid-faced Litchfield, succeeding in stopping the man so that he dropped with all the grace of a felled ox.

Justin's rescuer knelt down briefly beside the unconscious man before straightening, revealing himself to be Lord Bryan Anderson, Earl of Richmond, a fit and lithe gentleman of fifty years or so, the thickness of his hair prematurely white. 'Your right hook is as effective as ever, I see, Richmond,' Justin said admiringly.

'It would appear so.' The older man straightened the cuff of his shirt beneath his tailored black superfine as both men continued ignoring the inelegantly recumbent Litchfield. 'Dare I ask what you did that so annoyed the man?'

Justin shrugged. 'I allowed him to win at cards.'

'Indeed?' Richmond raised his brows. 'Considering the extent of his gambling debts, one would have thought he might have been more grateful.'

'One would have thought so, yes.' Justin watched unemotionally as the unconscious Litchfield was quietly removed from the club by two stoic-faced footmen. 'I thank you for your timely intervention, Richmond.'

'Think nothing of it, Royston.' The older man bowed.

Justin's top lip curled. 'So it would appear.'

Richmond nodded. 'I had the displeasure of serving in the army with him in India many years ago and know him to be a bully with a vicious temper. The men did not like him any more than his fellow officers did.'

'If that were the case, I am surprised one of them did not take steps to rid themselves of such a tyrant.' It was well known in army circles that the enlisted men—enlisted? Hah! They were usually men who had been forced into taking the king's shilling for one nefarious reason or another—occasionally chose to dispose of a particularly unpopular officer during the confusion of battle.

Richmond gave a rueful smile. 'That should have been the case, of course, and likely would have happened if he had lingered in the army overlong, but there was some indiscretion with another officer's wife, which caused his superior officer to see that he left India sooner rather than later.'

Justin studied the older man's bland expression for several seconds. 'And would that superior officer happen to have been yourself, sir?'

'It would,' Richmond said grimly.

'In that case I will bear your warning in mind,' Justin said. 'I wish you a good night, Richmond.' He lost no more time in making his departure as he proceeded out into the hallway to collect and don his hat and cloak in readiness for stepping outside.

'Hanover Square, if you please, Bilsbury,' he instructed his driver tersely as he climbed inside the ducal

length of muscled calf and thigh; he was without doubt the most handsome gentleman Ellie had ever beheld—

'Well?' he demanded even as he swept off his cloak and hat and handed them to Stanhope before striding across the vast hallway to where Ellie stood at the bottom of the wide and curving staircase.

—as well as being the most arrogant—

She drew in a breath. 'I sent a note earlier this evening requesting that you call—'

'Which is the very reason I am here now,' he cut in.

—and impatient!

And considering that Ellie had sent the note over two hours ago, she found his delayed response to that request to be less than helpful! 'I had expected you sooner…'

He stilled. 'Do I detect a measure of rebuke in your tone?'

Her cheeks felt warm at the underlying steel beneath the mildness of his tone. 'I—no…'

He relaxed his shoulders. 'I am gratified to hear it.'

Her chin rose determinedly. 'It is your grandmother whom I believe may have expected a more immediate response from you, your Grace.' Indeed, that dear lady had been asking every quarter of the hour, since she had requested Ellie, as her companion, to send a note to her grandson, as to whether or not there had been any word from him. The duke's arrival here now, so many hours after the note had been sent, was tardy to say the least.

'This is my immediate response.'

She raised red-gold brows. 'Indeed?'

Justin had no idea why it was he was even bothering to explain himself to this particular young woman. She was only a distant relative by marriage. Indeed, he could not remember even having spoken to Miss Eleanor Rosewood before now. He had noticed her, of course—bored and cynical he might be, but he was also a man!

Her hair was an intriguing shade of red, despite attempts on her part to mute its fieriness and curl in the severity of its style. Her eyes were a stunning clear green and surrounded by thick dark lashes, freckles sprinkled the tops of her creamy cheeks and the pertness of her tiny nose, and her mouth—

Ah, her mouth… Full and pouting, and naturally the colour of ripe strawberries, it was far too easy for a man to imagine such a mouth being put to far better uses than talking or eating!

She was tiny in both stature and figure, and yet the fullness of her breasts, visible above the neckline of her plain and unbecoming brown gown, emphasised the slenderness of her waist and thighs, her hands also tiny and delicate, the fingers long and slender in wrist-length cream lace gloves.

Justin was well aware that his grandmother had lost no time in gathering this orphaned chick into her own household as her companion after Eleanor had been left alone in the world, following the death of her mother and stepfather, Justin's own profligate cousin Frederick; Edith St Just might like to give the outward appearance of haughtiness and disdain, but to any who

Justin's impatience deepened. 'At which time I presume my grandmother asked that I be sent for?'

She nodded. 'She also requested that you go up to her bedchamber the moment you arrived.'

A request this lady had obviously forgotten to relay to him until now. Because his arrival had diverted her from the task, perhaps...? It was a possibility he found as intriguing as he did amusing.

He nodded. 'I will go up to her now. Perhaps you would arrange for some brandy to be brought to the library for when I return downstairs?'

'Of course.' Ellie found she was relieved to have something practical to do, her usual calm competence seeming to have deserted her the moment she found herself in Justin's overpoweringly masculine presence. 'Do you wish me to accompany you?'

The duke came to a halt on the second step of the wide staircase in order to turn and give her a pointed look. 'I believe I am well aware of where my grandmother's bedchamber is located, but you may accompany me up the stairs, to ensure I do not attempt to make away with the family silver, if that is your wish.'

'Is that "family silver" not already yours?' she asked, trying hard to keep hold of her composure against his needling.

'It is.' He smiled briefly. 'Then perhaps you fear I may become lost in my own house, Cousin?'

Ellie was well aware that this was his house. As was everything connected with the Duchy of Royston. 'I believe my time might be better served in seeking

dictated his own would be a marriage of convenience, rather than love. A marriage that would not exclude his children in the way that he had been excluded.

His three years as the Duke of Royston had ensured that he was denied nothing and certainly not any woman he expressed the least desire for—and, on several occasions, some he had not, such as other gentlemen's wives and the daughters of marriage-minded mamas!

Eleanor Rosewood, as companion to his grandmother, was not of that ilk, of course, just as their tenuous family connection ensured she could never be considered as Justin's social equal. At the same time, though, even that slight family connection meant he could not consider her as a future mistress, either. Frustrating, but true.

'Your Grace…?'

He frowned his irritation with her insistence on using his title. 'I believe we established only a few minutes ago that we are cousins of a sort and we should therefore address each other as Cousin Eleanor and Cousin Justin.'

Ellie's eyes widened in alarm at the mere thought of her using such familiarity with this rakishly handsome gentleman; Justin St Just, the twelfth Duke of Royston, was so top-lofty, so arrogantly haughty as he gave every appearance of looking down the length of his superior nose at the rest of the world, that Ellie would never be able to even think of him as a cousin, let alone address him as such.

Chapter Three

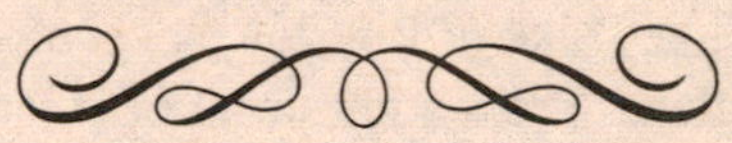

'I must say, you took your time getting here, Royston.'

Justin, as was the case with most men, was uncomfortable visiting a sickroom, but especially when it was that of his aged grandmother, the dowager duchess being a woman for whom he had the highest regard and affection.

Tonight, the pallor of her face emphasised each line and wrinkle, so that she looked every one of her almost seventy years as she lay propped up by white lace pillows piled high against the head of the huge four-poster bed. A state of affairs that was not in the least reassuring, despite the fact that her iron-grey hair was as perfectly styled as usual and her expression as proudly imperious.

The St Justs, as Justin knew only too well, after learning of his grandfather's long and private struggle with a wasting disease, were a breed apart when it came to bearing up under adversity; his grandmother might only be a St Just by marriage, but her strength of will was equal to, if not more than, any true-born St Just.

choose to spend their evenings? Many of the married ones, too!'

'I believe I may only be called young in years, Grandmama,' he drawled ruefully; these past three years as the Duke of Royston, and the onerous responsibilities of that title, had required that Justin become more circumspect in his public lifestyle, and at the same time they had left him little or no time for a private life either.

Perhaps it was time he thought seriously of acquiring a permanent mistress, a mild and biddable woman who would be only too pleased to attend to his needs, no matter what the time of day or night, but would make no demands of him other than that he keep her and provide a house in which they might meet. It was an idea that merited some further consideration.

But not here and now. 'I did not come here to discuss my own activities, when it is your own health which is currently in question.' he changed the subject deftly. 'Cousin Eleanor has informed me that Dr Franklyn was called to attend you earlier this evening. What is the problem, Grandmama?'

'Might I enquire when you decided that Ellie is to be referred to as your cousin?' Edith raised those imperious grey brows.

'Ellie?'

'Miss Eleanor Rosewood, your Cousin Frederick's stepdaughter, of course,' she supplied impatiently.

'I can hardly be so familiar as to address her as Ellie—a name I do not particularly care for, by the by—' Justin gave an irritated scowl '—when her mother, one

that restless manner and instead sit down in that chair beside me? It is making my head ache having to follow your movements in this way.' She gave a pained wince.

Only one part of that statement was of any relevance to Justin at this particular moment. 'In what way are you feeling unwell?' He pounced on the statement, his expression distracted as he lowered his long length down into the chair beside the bed before reaching out to take one of his grandmother's delicately fragile hands into both of his.

Edith gave a weary sigh. 'I find I become very tired of late. An occurrence which has made me realise that—it has made me aware that I should have made much more of an effort to ensure that things were settled before now…' She gave another sigh, a little mournful this time.

Justin scowled darkly. 'Grandmama, if this is yet another way for you to introduce the unwelcome subject of my acquiring a duchess—'

'Why, you conceited young whippersnapper!' She gave him a quelling glance as she sat up straighter in the bed. 'Contrary to what you appear to believe, I do not spend the whole of my waking life thinking up ways to entice my stubborn and uninterested grandson into matrimony!' Then she seemed to collect herself and settled back once more on her pillows with another pained wince.

Justin gave a rueful shake of his head at hearing her berate him so soundly; not too many people would have dared speak to him like that and hope to get away with

child, had, as a consequence, meant that it was Justin's paternal grandparents, Edith and George St Just, who were the constant influences in his life, and with whom he had chosen to spend the majority of his school holidays, as well as Christmas and birthdays.

'Doctor Franklyn is of the opinion that I am simply wearing out—'

'Utterly ridiculous!' Justin barked, sitting forwards tensely, blue gaze fierce as he searched the unusual delicate pallor of her face. 'He is mistaken. Why, you had tea with your two dear friends only a few days ago, attended Lady Huntsley's ball with them just yesterday evening—'

'As a consequence, today I am feeling so weak that I do not even have the energy to rise from my bed.'

'You have overtaxed yourself, that is all,' he insisted.

'Justin, you are no longer a child and, sadly, neither am I.' His grandmother gave another heavy sigh. 'And I cannot say I will not be pleased to be with your grandfather again—'

'I refuse to listen to this nonsense a moment longer!' Justin released her hand to stand up before glowering down at her. 'I will speak to Dr Franklyn myself.'

'Do so, by all means, if you feel you must, but bullying the doctor cannot make me any younger than I am,' Edith reasoned gently.

Justin drew in a sharp breath at the truth of that statement. 'Perhaps you might rally, find new purpose, if I were to reconsider my decision not to marry in the near future.'

year, and Justin had not so much as spared a thought for the possibility of her dying just yet; Edith St Just had been, and still was, the woman in his life on whom he had always depended, a woman of both iron will and indomitable spirit, always there, the steely matriarch of the St Just family.

'May we discuss Eleanor's future now, Justin?' Edith continued, uncharacteristically meek.

Eleanor Rosewood, and her future, were the last things that Justin wished to discuss at this moment, but a single glance at his grandmother's face was enough to silence his protests as he noticed once again how the paleness of her face, and the shadows beneath her eyes, gave her the appearance of being every one of those eight and sixty years.

He bit back the sharpness of his reply and instead resumed his seat beside the bed. 'Very well, Grandmama, if you insist, then let us talk of Cousin Eleanor's future.'

She nodded. 'It is my dearest wish to see her comfortably married before I dep—am no longer here,' she corrected at Justin's scowl.

He raised his brows. 'It seems to me that you appear to wish this dubious state upon all those close to you. I am heartily relieved it is not just me you have set your sights on.'

'Do not be facetious, Royston!' The dowager frowned. 'As I have already stated, you must do as you wish where your own future bride is concerned, but for a young woman in Ellie's position, marriage is the only solution.'

some such into offering her marriage?' he suggested sarcastically.

'The dowry would certainly be a start.' His grandmother took his suggestion seriously as she nodded slowly. 'Heaven knows the Royston fortune is large enough you would not even notice its loss! But I do not see why Eleanor should have to settle for an impoverished clergyman. Surely, somewhere amongst your acquaintances, you must know of a titled gentleman or two who would willingly overlook her social shortcomings in order to take to wife a young woman of personal fortune, who also happens to be the stepcousin of the powerful Duke of Royston?'

Justin had meant to tease with his suggestion of a providing a dowry for Eleanor, but he could see by the seriousness of his grandmother's expression that she, at least, was in deadly earnest. 'Let me see if I understand you correctly, Grandmama. You wish for me to first settle a sizeable dowry upon your companion, before then seeking out and securing a suitable, preferably titled husband, for her amongst my acquaintances?' The suggestion was not only preposterous, but seemed slightly incestuous to Justin in view of his own less than cousinly thoughts about that young lady just minutes ago!

'I do not expect you to approach the subject quite so callously, Royston.' Edith eyed him impatiently. 'I am very fond of the gel and I should not like to see her married to a man she did not like, or whom did not like her.'

His brows rose. 'So you are, in fact, expecting me to

when the lid was lifted! 'I believe your current indisposition has addled your brain, Grandmama!' He shook his head. 'I do not attend music soirées or balls in the normal course of events, let alone with the intention of marrying off my young stepcousin to some unsuspecting gentleman!'

'But there is nothing to say that you could not make the exception in these special circumstances, is there?' she insisted defiantly.

'No, of course there is not. But—'

'It would make me very happy if you were to do so, Justin.'

He narrowed suddenly suspicious blue eyes on the supposedly frail figure of his grandmother as she once again lay back, so small and vulnerable-looking against those snowy white pillows. 'I thought it was Cousin Eleanor's happiness which was your first and only concern?'

'It is.' Edith's eyes snapped her irritation at his perspicacity. 'And I can think of no better way to secure that happiness than you publicly acknowledging Ellie as a favoured cousin.'

'A favoured cousin of such low social standing she has been in your own employ this past year,' he reminded her drily.

'I very much doubt that any of the *ton* would make the connection between that mousy young woman and Miss Eleanor Rosewood, the elegant and beautiful cousin of the Duke of Royston.'

He very much doubted the truth of that claim, in re-

Justin had the uncomfortable feeling that somewhere in the course of this conversation he had not only been manipulated, but soundly outmanoeuvred. An unusual occurrence, admittedly, but somehow his grandmother seemed to have succeeded in doing so. He—

'There is one other subject upon which I shall require your assistance, my boy.'

He eyed the redoubtable old lady extremely warily now. 'Yes?'

'I believe it might be advisable, before any marriage were to take place, to attempt to ascertain the identity of Ellie's real father…'

Justin's eyes widened in shock. 'Her *real* father? Was that not Mr Rosewood, then?'

'As that gentleman had already been dead for a full year before Ellie was born, I do not believe so, no…' Edith grimaced.

This situation, one not even of Justin's own choosing, suddenly became more and more surreal. 'And is Eleanor herself aware of that fact?'

His grandmother gave a snort. 'Of course she is not. I only discovered the truth of things myself when I had her mother investigated after that idiot Frederick ran off to Gretna Green so impetuously and married the woman.'

'So my stepcousin and ward is not only penniless, but is also a bastard—'

'Royston!'

Justin groaned out loud. 'And if I should discover

one of Ellie's romantic dreams, both day and night this past year, to a degree that she believed herself half in love with him already.

Which made awaiting his appearance in the library now even more excruciatingly nerve-racking. How embarrassing if she were to reveal, by look, word or deed, even an inkling of the sensual fantasies she had woven so romantically about the powerful and handsome duke! Fantasies that made Ellie's cheeks burn just to think of them as she imagined Justin returning her feelings for him, resulting in those chiselled lips claiming her own, those long and elegant hands caressing her back, before moving higher, to cup the fullness of her eagerly straining breasts—

'Your thoughts appear to please you, Cousin Eleanor...?'

Ellie gave a guilty start as she rose hastily from the chair beside the fireplace to turn and face the man whose lips and hands she had just been imagining touching her with such intimacy.

Justin did not at all care for the look of apprehension which appeared upon Eleanor Rosewood's delicately blushing face as she rose to gaze across the library at him. Apprehension, accompanied by a certain amount of guilt, if he was not mistaken. What she had to feel guilty about he had no idea, nor did he care for that look of apprehension either. 'Perhaps not,' he drawled as he stepped further into the room and closed the door behind him before crossing to where the decanter of brandy and glasses had been placed upon the desktop.

Justin felt a sudden urge, a strong desire, to kiss each and every one of them! He determinedly brought those wayward thoughts to an abrupt end and his mouth compressed. 'My grandmother has requested that you…assist her in the matter of the ball.'

Her little pink tongue moved moistly across those full and pouting lips, making him shift uncomfortably. 'I am not sure what assistance I could possibly be in the planning of such a grand occasion, but I shall of course endeavour to offer the dowager duchess whatever help I am able.'

Justin gave her an amused look. 'You misunderstand, Cousin Eleanor—the assistance required of you is that you attend the Royston Ball.'

She nodded. 'And I have already said that I shall be only too pleased to help the dowager duchess in any way that I can—'

'You are to attend the ball as her guest—careful!' he warned as the brandy glass looked in danger of slipping from her fingers.

Ellie's fingers immediately tightened about the bulbous glass even as stared up at him in disbelief. Justin could not seriously be suggesting that she was to attend the ball as a member of the *ton,* was he?

The implacability of his expression as he looked at her down the long length of his aristocratic nose appeared to suggest that he was.

Ellie knew that to be an erroneous statement from the onset; if Justin listened without argument to everything his grandmother said to him, then he would have long since found himself married, with half-a-dozen heirs in the nursery! For Edith St Just made no secret of her desire to see her grandson acquire his duchess, and not long afterwards begin producing his heirs. A desire which Ellie knew he had successfully evaded fulfilling during this past year, at least.

Ellie looked up at him from beneath lowered lashes as she tried to gauge the duke's response to his grandmother's unexpected decision to invite her lowly companion to attend the prestigious Royston Ball. A fruitless task, as it happened, the blandness of Justin's expression revealing absolutely none of that arrogant gentleman's inner thoughts. Although Ellie thought she detected a slight glint of amusement in the depths of those deep blue eyes… No doubt at her expense, she thought irritably.

Ellie was not a fool and she might well consider herself half in love with Justin, and find him exciting in a forbidden way, but that did not preclude her from knowing he was also arrogant, cynical and mocking. Or that his mockery on this occasion was directed towards her.

She drew in a ragged breath in an attempt to steady herself. 'I shall, of course, explain to her Grace, first thing in the morning, exactly why it is I cannot accept her invitation.'

'And I wish you every success with that.' There was

'Even you?' she couldn't help asking, then flushed at her own temerity.

Justin frowned at this second attempt on Eleanor's part to ascertain his own views on the subject. Especially when he was now unsure of those views himself...

Admittedly, he had initially dismissed the very idea of her introduction into society, but second, and perhaps third thoughts, had revealed to him that it was not such an unacceptable idea as he had first considered. His grandmother's argument, in favour of doing so, in an effort to secure Eleanor a suitable husband, although a considerable inconvenience to himself, was perfectly valid. Most especially if Justin were to provide Eleanor with a suitable dowry, as his grandmother suggested he must do.

Eleanor was both ladylike in her appearance as well as her manner. The fact that she also happened to be impoverished should not prevent her from seeking the same happiness in the marriage mart as any other young lady of nineteen years.

There was that irritating question as to whom Eleanor's real father might be, of course, but Justin had his grandmother's assurances that Eleanor knew nothing of that, believing herself to be the daughter of Mr Henry Rosewood. And if Justin's investigations into that matter, at his grandmother's behest, should prove otherwise, then who needed to be any the wiser about it?

The father, perhaps, if he did not already know of his daughter's existence...

phasising the fullness of those creamy breasts. 'I am sure I am very…gratified by her Grace's concern—'

'Are you?'

Ellie gave Justin a quick glance beneath lowered lashes as she heard the mocking amusement in his tone; grateful as she was to the dowager duchess for coming to her rescue a year ago, it had not been an easy task for Ellie to learn to hold her impetuous tongue, or keep her fiery temper in check, as was befitting in the companion of a much older lady and a dowager duchess at that, and they were faults her mother had been at pains to point out to Ellie on a regular basis when she was alive.

The duke's amusement, so obviously at her expense, which she once again saw in those intense blue eyes, was enough to make Ellie forget all of her previous caution, as she snapped waspishly, 'I am gratified to see that at least one of us finds this situation amusing and it is not me!'

'If nothing else, it has at least succeeded in diverting my grandmother's attention from my own lack of interest in the married state!' he lobbed back lazily.

Ellie eyed him in frustration. 'I am no more interested in entering into marriage, simply because it's convenient, than you are!'

Her mother's marriage, to a youngest son, had resulted in Muriel Rosewood being left a virtually impoverished and expectant widow on Henry Rosewood's death, with only a small yearly stipend from the Rosewood family coffers, and no other interest in the widow

He lifted a brow. 'Because it would make my grandmother happy if I did?'

Ellie continued to look up at him for several long seconds, a stare the duke met with unblinking and bored implacability. Bored?

So he found the idea of marrying her off, whether she wished it or not, whether she would be happy or not, to be not only amusing but boring as well?

And to think—to imagine that she had thought only minutes ago that she was in love with Justin St Just! So much so, that she had awaited with trepidation the announcement of his betrothal and forthcoming marriage to some beautiful and highly eligible young lady. Now she could not help but feel pity for whichever of those unlucky women should eventually be chosen as duchess to this arrogant man!

Indeed, as far as Ellie was concerned, Justin St Just had become nothing more than her tormentor, out to bedevil her with threats of arranging her marriage to a man she neither knew nor loved.

It could not be allowed to happen!

Except…Ellie had no idea how she was to go about avoiding such an unwanted outcome when the duke and the dowager duchess, both so imperious and determined, seemed so set upon the idea.

She placed her brandy glass down upon one of the side tables before commencing to pace the room, as she feverishly sought for ways in which she might avoid the state of an arranged, unhappy marriage, without upset-

Could it be—did Eleanor's tastes perhaps run in another direction entirely? No, surely not! It would be a cruelty on the part of Mother Nature if a woman of such understated beauty, and surprisingly fiery a temperament as Eleanor, was not destined to occupy the arms, the bed, of some lucky gentleman. In other circumstances, she would almost certainly have made the perfect mistress—

No, he really must not think of her in such terms. He must in future consider himself as purely a guardian where she was concerned.

Even if his extremely private inner thoughts strayed constantly in the opposite direction!

'Have you drawn any conclusions yet as to how you might thwart my grandmother's plans for your immediate future?' Justin teased after several long minutes of her pacing. 'If so, I wish you would share them with me, if only for my own future reference?'

Ellie came to an abrupt halt to glare across the library at the lazily reclining form of the relaxed duke, the glow from the flames of the fire turning his fashionably styled hair a rich and burnished gold, those patrician features thrown into stark and cruel relief, and causing Ellie's pulse to quicken in spite of herself.

The rapidity of her pulse, and sudden shortness of breath, told her that, although she now doubted herself in love with him any more, she was still not completely averse to his physical attributes, at least.

His arrogance and mockery, when directly aimed

now a cold and glittering sapphire blue. 'There you are wrong, Eleanor,' he rasped. 'My own feelings on that particular subject are in total opposition to your own,' he elaborated harshly as she raised questioning brows, 'in that I would never consider marrying anyone who declared a love for me, or vice versa.'

Ellie's eyes widened at his words and the coldness of the tone in which he said them. She had believed that the duke's aversion to marriage was because he had not yet met the woman whom he loved enough to make his duchess. His statement now showed it was the opposite.

Ellie could not help but wonder why…

She was aware, of course, that many marriages in the *ton* were made for financial or social gain, as her mother's had been to Frederick St Just. But often the couples in those marriages learnt a respect and affection for each other, and in some cases love itself. Again, that had not happened in her mother's case, her marriage to Frederick, an inveterate gambler and womaniser, tolerable at best, painful at worst, certainly colouring Ellie's own views on the subject.

But for any gentleman to deliberately state his intention of never feeling love for his wife, or to have her feel love for him, seemed harsh in the extreme.

And surely it was asking too much of any woman, if married to Justin St Just, not to fall in love with him?

Or perhaps the answer to his stated aversion to loving his future wife had something to do with why he could not initially be found earlier on this evening…?

Ellie knew that many gentlemen of the *ton* had mis-

Justin grimaced. 'You are an optimist as well as a romantic, I see.'

A faint flush darkened her cheeks even as she raised her chin proudly. 'I would hope I am a realist, your Grace.'

He gave a slow shake of his head. 'A realist would know to accept when she is defeated.'

'A realist would accept, even with your generous offer of providing me with a dowry, that I am not meant to be a part of society. Indeed,' she continued firmly as he would have spoken, 'I have no ambitions to ever be so.'

Justin raised his brows. 'You consider us a frivolous lot, then, with nothing to recommend us?'

He found himself the focus of dark-green eyes as Eleanor studied him unblinkingly for several seconds before giving a brief, dismissive smile. 'There is no answer I could give to that question which would not result in my either insulting you or denigrating myself. As such, I choose to make no reply at all.'

It was, Justin realised admiringly, both a clever and witty answer, and delivered in so ambiguous a tone as to render it as being at least one of the things she claimed it was not meant to be!

Again he found himself entertained by this surprisingly outspoken young woman, to appreciate why his grandmother was so fond of her; Edith St Just did not suffer twittering fools any more gladly than he did himself.

He gave her a courtly bow. 'I greatly look forward to

Justin's smile widened at her stubborn optimism. 'I do not believe there is any way in which you might prevent it—other than your possibly falling down the stairs and breaking a leg before then!' He laughed in earnest as he saw by Eleanor's furrowed brow that she was actually giving the suggestion serious consideration. 'Would it really be such a bad thing to be seen entering the ballroom on my arm, Eleanor?' he chided softly as he crossed the room to stand in front of her. 'If so, then you are not in the least flattering to a man's ego.'

'I do not believe your own ego to be in need of flattery,' Ellie murmured huskily, totally disconcerted by Justin's sudden and close proximity. Indeed, she could feel the warmth of his breath ruffling those errant curls at her temple.

'No?' Long lean fingers reached up to smooth back those curls, the touch of his fingers light and cool against the heat of her brow.

Ellie swallowed before attempting an answer, at the same time inwardly willing her voice to sound as it normally did. 'How can it, when you are the elusive but much-coveted prize of the marriage mart?'

She sounded only a little breathless, she realised thankfully, at the same time as she knew her disobedient knees were in danger of turning to water and no longer supporting her.

'Am I?' A smile tilted those sculptured lips as those lean fingers now trailed lightly down the warmth of her cheek.

like my grandmother, believe my delay in arriving here this evening to be because I was in the arms of my current mistress,' he said speculatively.

Ellie felt her cheeks flush even warmer, no doubt once again clashing horribly with the red of her hair, as well as emphasising the freckles across her cheeks and nose that had long been the bane of her life. 'I am not in the least interested as to the reason for the delay in your arrival—'

'Oh, but I think you are, Eleanor,' he contradicted softly. 'Very interested.'

She gave a pained frown as she looked up into those intent blue eyes and decided she had suffered quite enough of this gentleman's teasing for one evening. 'Is your conceit so great that you believe every woman you meet must instantly fall under the spell of your charm?'

'Not in the least.' Those blue eyes now twinkled down at her merrily. 'But it is gratifying to know that you at least find me charming, Eleanor—'

'What I *believe,* your Grace, is that you are a conceited ass—' She fell abruptly silent as Justin lowered his head and bit lightly, reprovingly, on her bottom lip.

Ellie stiffened as if frozen in place and her heart seemed to cease beating altogether as she acknowledged that the coldly arrogant Duke of Royston, the mockingly handsome Justin St Just, had just run the moistness of his sensuous tongue over her parted lips…

would be as well if you desisted from challenging me by insulting me?' he added harshly in a desperate attempt to divert her attention away from his despicable behaviour.

'You—I—' Ellie gasped her indignation, eyes wide and accusing at the unfairness of being blamed for his shockingly familiar behaviour. She now wrenched completely out of his grasp to glare up at him. 'You are worse than conceited, sir! You are nothing more than—'

'Yes, yes,' he dismissed in a bored voice, knowing he had to carry on now as he had started. 'I have no doubt I am a rake and a cad, and many other unpleasant things, in your innocent eyes.' He eyed her mockingly as he straightened the lace cuffs of his shirt beneath his jacket. 'You will need to be a little more subtle, my dear, if you are to learn to rebuff the advances of the gentlemen of the *ton* without also insulting them.'

'And why should I care whether they feel insulted, if they have dared to take the same liberties you just did?' Ellie asked scornfully.

'Because it is part of the game, Eleanor,' he explained, hoping she would believe him.

She stilled, eyes narrowed. 'Game…?'

He gave a slight inclination of his head. 'How else is a man to know whether or not he likes a woman enough to marry her, let alone bed her, if he does not first flirt with her and take a liberty or two?'

She breathed shallowly. 'You are saying that you—that your reason for—for making love to me just now was your way of preparing me for the advances of other gentlemen?'

Blond brows rose in disbelief. 'Are you *dismissing* me, Eleanor?'

Her mouth set stubbornly as she refused to be cowed by his haughty arrogance. 'Did it sound as if I were?'

'Yes.'

She gave a small smile of her own. 'Then that is what I must have been doing.'

Justin gave a surprised bark of laughter at the same time as he cursed the fact that he had realised only this evening that he found this particular young woman so damned entertaining. It was, to say the least, inconvenient, if not downright dangerous, to his peace of mind, if nothing else. As he had realised when he had kissed her just now. A mistake on his part, which Justin had felt it necessary to explain by dismissing it as a lesson for Eleanor's future reference—even if the lesson *he* had learnt had been not to kiss her again. 'I am a duke, Eleanor, you are an impoverished stepcousin; as such it is not permissible for you to dismiss me.'

She raised auburn brows. 'Another lesson in social etiquette, your Grace?'

Gods, this woman had enough pride and audacity to tempt any man— Justin brought those thoughts to an abrupt halt, a scowl darkening his brow as he looked down at her between narrowed lids. 'One of many ahead of me, I fear,' he taunted. 'Your social skills appear to have been sadly neglected, my dear.' And he, Justin acknowledged bleakly, would have to take great care in future not to 'enjoy' those lessons too much!

Colour blazed in Eleanor's cheeks at his deliberate

impulse he felt to reach out and clasp her by the shoulders before soundly shaking her. After which he would probably be tempted into pulling her into his arms and kissing her once again. And heaven—or more likely hell—only knew where that might lead! 'For now,' he bit out between clenched teeth.

She turned and made good her escape, closing the library door softly behind her.

Leaving Justin with the unpleasant knowledge that he might have given his grandmother's companion little thought until this evening—apart from noticing those kissable lips and the tempting swell of her breasts like any other red-blooded male would!—but he was now far too aware of the physical attributes, and the amusement to be derived from the sharp tongue, of one Miss Eleanor Rosewood.

'Would you care to explain to me exactly why it is I am out riding with you in the park this afternoon, your Grace, chaperoned by her Grace's own maid…' Ellie glanced back to where poor Mary was currently being bounced and jostled about in the dowager duchess's least best carriage '…when I am sure my time might be better occupied in helping her Grace with the last-minute preparations for the Royston Ball later this evening?' She shot the duke a questioning glance as she rode beside him perched atop the docile chestnut mare he had requested be saddled for her use.

His chiselled lips were curved into a humourless smile, blue eyes narrowed beneath his beaver hat, his

trated and none the wiser for having visited, and spoken with, the good Dr Franklyn.

His evenings had been no more enjoyable, spent at one gaming hell or another, usually with the result that he had arrived back at his rooms in the late hours or early morning, nursing a full purse, but also a raging headache from inhaling too much of other gentlemen's cigar smoke and drinking far too much of the club's brandy. Last night had been no exception, resulting in Justin having risen only hours ago from his bed. He had then had to rush through his toilet in order that he might be ready to go riding in the park with Eleanor at the fashionable time of five o'clock.

An occurrence which had made him regret ever having agreed to his grandmother's request today. 'My own wishes are unimportant at this time,' he dismissed flatly.

Eleanor eyed him with a slight frown. 'I had thought her Grace seems slightly improved these past few days?'

Justin gave her a rueful glance, having no intention of discussing his grandmother's health with this young woman, or anyone else. 'You believe my grandmother's possible ill health to be the only reason I would have consented to ride in the park with you?'

Eleanor shrugged slender shoulders, her appearance thoroughly enchanting today in a fashionable green-velvet riding habit and matching bonnet, the red of her curls peaking enticingly from beneath the brim of that bonnet. 'You obviously have a deep regard for your grandmother's happiness, your Grace.'

nance showed he was obviously as reluctant to be here as she was!

'No, I would not,' she now answered him firmly.

Once again Justin found it impossible not to laugh out loud at her honesty. 'Even though, as I have previously stated, it is well known amongst the *ton* that I never escort young ladies, in the park or anywhere else?'

'Even then,' she stated firmly. 'Indeed, I do not know how you manage to stand all the gawking and gossiping which has taken place since we arrived here together.'

Justin raised surprised brows as he turned to look about them. Having been lost in his own sleep-deprived drink-induced misery until now, he had taken little note of any interest being shown in them.

An interest that became far less overt when openly challenged by his icy-blue gaze. 'Ignore it, as I do,' he advised dismissively as he turned back to the young woman riding beside him.

Green eyes widened in the pallor of Eleanor's face. 'I find that somewhat impossible to do.'

'Perhaps a compliment or two might help divert you?' he mused. 'I should have told you earlier what a capable horsewoman you so obviously are.' Far too accomplished for the docile mount he had allocated to her. A horse, Justin now realised, whose chestnut coat was very similar in colouring to the red of her hair.

'Are you so surprised?' she taunted before giving him a rueful smile. 'My stepfather, your own cousin Frederick, may have been offhand in his attentions,

fore as quickly being dismissed in favour of him looking down the length of his nose at her with his usual haughty arrogance. 'Will your own mother be attending the ball this evening?' she prompted curiously, not having met Rachel St Just as yet.

Her son scowled darkly. 'My mother never leaves her country estate.'

'Never?'

'Never.'

He answered so coldly, so uncompromisingly, it was impossible for Ellie not to comprehend that his mother was a subject he preferred not to discuss. Not that she was going to let that stand in her way! 'Was your own parents' marriage an unhappy one?'

'Far from it,' he rasped. 'They loved each other to the exclusion of all else,' he added harshly.

To the exclusion of their only child? she pondered, slightly shocked. And, if so, did that also explain his own views on the married state? It was—

'Good Gad, Royston, what a shock to see your illustrious self out and about in the park!'

Ellie forgot her musings as she turned to look at the man who so obviously greeted the duke with false joviality. A gentleman who might once have been handsome, but whose florid face and heavy jowls now rendered him as being far from attractive, and his obesity was obviously a great trial to the brown horse upon which he sat.

'No more so than you, Litchfield,' Justin answered the other man languidly, causing Ellie to look at him

mottled face, wisps of auburn hair, liberally streaked with grey, peeping out from beneath his hat and brushing the soiled collar of his shirt.

'Indeed,' Ellie confirmed coolly.

'If you would care to…ride, another afternoon, then I should be only too pleased to offer my services as…your escort. You have only to send word to my home in Russell Square. Lord Dryden Litchfield is the name.'

The man's familiar manner and address, considering the two of them had not so much as been formally introduced—deliberately so, on Justin's part?—were such that even Eleanor recognised it as being far from acceptable in fashionable circles. As she also recognised that Lord Litchfield was far from being a gentleman. Which begged the question as to how Justin came to be acquainted with such an unpleasant man.

'I will join you shortly, Eleanor,' Justin bit out harshly.

'Your Grace?' she said in surprise as, having turned her horse back in the direction they had just come, she now realised he had made no effort to accompany her, the two men currently seeming to be engaged in an ocular battle of wills.

A battle of wills she had no doubt the duke would ultimately win, but it was one which Ellie would prefer not take place at all; not only would it be unpleasant to herself, but she very much doubted the dowager duchess would be at all pleased to learn that Ellie had been present during an altercation in the park between her grandson and another gentleman.

man gave him a speculatively look. 'Can this be the same young lady whose missive caused you to end our card game so that you could run eagerly to her side?'

Eleanor's note was indeed responsible for that occurrence, but certainly not in the way in which Litchfield implied it had.

'Ah, I see that it is indeed the case.' Litchfield nodded in satisfaction at Justin's silence. 'As I said, she is certainly a rare beauty—'

'And as I have said, she is not for the likes of you,' Justin bit out tautly.

'Well, well.' The older man eyed him curiously. 'Can it be that the top-lofty Duke of Royston has finally met his match? Are we to expect an announcement soon?'

'You are to *expect* that I shall not be pleased if I hear you have made so much as a single personal remark or innuendo about the young lady who is my ward,' Justin snarled, wanting nothing more than to take this insolent cur by the throat and squeeze until the breath left his body. Either that, or take a whip to him. And Justin would cheerfully have done either of those things, if he had not known it would draw unwanted attention to Eleanor.

Litchfield's eyes widened. 'Your ward...?'

Justin gave a haughty nod. 'Indeed.'

The other man continued to look at him searchingly for several seconds before giving a shout of derisive laughter and then turning to look at Eleanor speculatively once again. 'How very interesting...' He raised a mocking gloved hand to his temple before turning

'We have shared a card game or two, which he has invariably lost.' Justin shrugged dismissively. 'His reputation is such that much of society shuns him. And while we are on the subject,' he added harshly, 'I forbid you to so much as acknowledge him should you ever chance to meet him again.'

'You *forbid* it?' Ellie gasped incredulously.

The duke looked implacably at her. 'I do, yes. Unless, of course, I am mistaken and you would welcome Litchfield's attentions?'

She gave another shudder just recalling that unpleasant man. 'Of course I would not.'

'Then—'

'Whilst I accept that we are distantly related by marriage, *Cousin*—' Ellie's bland tone revealed none of her inner anger at his high-handedness '—and that you are the grandson of my employer—'

'—and your newly appointed guardian—'

'Perhaps that is so—'

'There is no perhaps about it!' the duke swiftly interjected.

'Even so, I cannot—I simply cannot allow you to forbid, or allow, any of my future actions,' Ellie informed him firmly, with far too many memories of how his cousin Frederick had held such sway over her poor mother for the last years of her life.

Justin reached out and grasped the reins of her horse as she would have urged her horse into a canter. 'In this instance I must insist you obey me, Eleanor.'

Tears of anger now blurred her vision. 'You may

Chapter Six

'I believe, Royston, that if you do not cease scowling, you are in danger of taking your duties as Ellie's guardian to such a degree that you will succeed in scaring away all but the most determined of eligible young gentlemen!'

Justin turned to raise one arrogant brow as he looked down to where his grandmother had moved to stand beside him at the edge of the crowded dance floor in her candlelit ballroom. Still slightly pale, and uncharacteristically fragile in her demeanour, the dowager duchess had, as she had said she would, rallied from her sickbed in order to take her place as hostess of the Royston Ball.

Justin's mood had not improved since he and Eleanor had parted so frostily upon returning to the stables behind Royston House. For the most part because Justin knew he had handled the situation badly, that issuing orders to a woman as stubborn as Eleanor was proving to be was sure to result in her doing the exact opposite of what was being asked of her—an accusation, which if

lobes of her ears, the creamy expanse of her throat and breasts, were all completely unadorned.

As a consequence, Justin realised that Eleanor Rosewood's understated elegance gave her the appearance of a dove amongst garishly adorned peacocks. A pure, unblemished, perfectly cut diamond set amongst roughly hewn and gaudy-coloured sapphires, emeralds and rubies.

As predicted, the crowded ballroom had fallen deathly silent the moment Stanhope had announced their entrance. But Justin was fully aware the speculative attention was not directed solely towards him this evening, but included the young lady standing so coolly self-contained at his side—admittedly, it was a façade of calm only, as hinted at by the slight trembling of her gloved hand as it rested lightly upon his arm, but to all outward appearances Eleanor was a picture of composure and elegance. She was also, as his grandmother had intended, instantly recognised as the same young woman who had been seen riding in the park with him this afternoon.

The ladies, as Eleanor had previously suggested might be the case, had gazed openly and critically at her from behind fluttering fans—with not a single sign of recognition, Justin noted ruefully, that the elegant Miss Eleanor Rosewood was also Ellie, the previously nondescript companion of the dowager duchess. The gentlemen, Justin had noted with more annoyance, had been much more open in their admiration.

An admiration confirmed by the fact that at least a

something amusing her current dance partner had said to her. 'Lord Braxton can hardly be considered young or entirely eligible,' he remarked curtly to his grandmother.

'Nonsense!' Edith dismissed as she continued to smile benevolently at her young protégée. 'Jeremy Caulfield is a widower as well as being an earl.'

Justin grimaced. 'He is also twice Eleanor's age and in need of a stepmother for all of those children he keeps hidden away in the nursery at Caulfield Park!'

His grandmother raised iron-grey brows. 'There are but three children, Justin, the heir, the spare and a girl. And anyone with eyes in their head can see that Braxton is smitten with Ellie herself, rather than having any thoughts of providing his children with another mother.'

Justin was only too well aware that Jeremy Caulfield's admiration of Eleanor was personal; that was made more than obvious by the warm way the other man gazed upon her so intently, and the way in which Caulfield's hand had lingered upon hers as they'd danced together. That Eleanor returned his liking was obvious in the relaxed and natural way in which she returned the earl's smiles and conversation. Nor could Justin deny, inwardly at least, that it would be a very good match for Eleanor if Caulfield were to become seriously enamoured of her, enough so that he made her an offer of marriage.

It would, Justin also acknowledged, bring a quick end to his reluctant role as Eleanor's guardian.

have contemplated agreeing to it if not for his deep regard for Edith and that lady's recent bout of ill health.

Thankfully, the dowager duchess really had seemed to improve a little over the last few days, and although she was still pale, she gave every appearance of enjoying the evening; Ellie knew that dear lady well enough by now to know that Edith St Just would never admit to it if she were not!

The Earl of Braxton looked genuinely disappointed by Ellie's refusal to sit with him at supper. 'Perhaps if I were to ask the dowager duchess's permission—'

'As Miss Rosewood is my own ward, it is my permission you would need to receive, Braxton,' the cold voice of Justin St Just cut in.

The older man turned, a pleasant smile curving his lips. 'Then perhaps you might consent to allowing me to escort Miss Rosewood into supper, Royston?'

'I am afraid that would not do at all, Braxton.' The duke looked down the length of his nose at the other man.

'Oh, but—'

'It will not do, Eleanor,' Justin repeated firmly as she started to protest. 'Forgive my ward, Braxton.' He turned back to the earl. 'I am afraid Eleanor is new to society. As such she is unaware of the attention she has already drawn to herself by her naivety and flirtatiousness.'

Ellie's eyes widened at the unfairness of the accusation. Admittedly she had not sat down for a single dance since that first one with Justin, but she believed that her

pale her cheeks had now become, those freckles more evident on her nose and cheeks, and that there were tears glistening in those deep-green eyes as she looked up at him reproachfully.

Damn it to hell!

He forced himself to slow his angry strides and loosen his tight grip upon her arm before speaking again. 'It may not appear so, Eleanor,' he explained, also attempting to soften the harshness of his tone, 'but I assure you I am only acting in your best interests. For you to have singled Braxton out so soon, by eating supper alone with him, would have been as good as a declaration on your part.'

A puzzled frown marred her creamy brow as she blinked back the tears. 'A declaration? Of what, exactly?'

'Of your willingness to accept a marriage proposal from him should one be forthcoming.'

'That is utterly ridiculous…' she recoiled with a horrified gasp '…when I have only just been introduced to him!' If anything her face had grown even paler.

Justin nodded grimly. 'And being new to society, you are as yet unaware of the subtle nuances of courtship.'

She shook her head, red curls bouncing against the slenderness of her creamy nape. 'But I am sure the earl meant no such familiarity by his supper invitation. He merely wished to continue our discussion, to learn my views, on the merits or otherwise, of engaging a companion or governess for his five-year-old daughter.'

consulting with you on what is best for the future education of his young, motherless daughter?'

Ellie gave a pained frown. 'Well…yes.'

Had she been naïve in taking Lord Caulfield's conversation at face value? She had not thought so at the time, but Justin knew the ways of society far better than she, after all. Yet it had seemed such a harmless conversation, Jeremy Caulfield so terribly bewildered and at a loss as to how best to bring up a little girl on his own—

Oh, good lord…!

'I believe my evening has now been quite ruined!' Ellie almost felt as if she might quite happily sit down and cry rather than attempt to eat any of the delicious supper laid out so temptingly before her.

Justin gave her a humourless smile. 'Do not take on so, Eleanor, a single inappropriate conversation with a gentleman does not commit you to spending a lifetime with him. Indeed, I should not give my permission for such a marriage even if such an offer were forthcoming. And I have no doubt my grandmother is even now excusing your behaviour by reiterating to Braxton your inexperience in such matters.'

'And that makes me feel so much better!' Ellie snapped, her earlier feelings of well-being having completely dissipated during the course of this conversation.

She had believed herself to be doing so well, to be behaving with all the dignity and decorum as befitted the supposed ward of the Duke of Royston, and instead it now seemed she had been encouraging the Earl of

in total contradiction to her own. He thought it was far better to marry a woman for her lineage and ability to produce healthy children. On which subject… 'And what of children, Eleanor?' he enquired. 'Do you have no desire to have a son or daughter of your own one day?'

Green eyes twinkled mischievously as she looked about them pointedly, the supper room now filling with other members of the *ton* seeking refreshment. 'Is our present conversation not as socially unacceptable as discussing the education of Lord Caulfield's young daughter with him?' she murmured softly before leaning forwards to pierce a piece of juicy pineapple with a fork and lifting it up to her lips.

'Perhaps,' Justin allowed ruefully. Then he found himself unable to look away from the fullness of her lips as they closed about the juicy fruit.

Her expression was thoughtful as she chewed and swallowed the fruit before innocently licking the excess juice from the plumpness of her lips. 'Then of course I would dearly love to have children of my own one day, both a son and a daughter at least. But only—'

'If you were to have those children with "a man who loved you with all of his heart",' he finished drily.

Ellie smiled. 'Why are you so cynical about falling in love, your Grace…? Your Grace?' she prompted quizzically as he started laughing again.

He raised an eyebrow. 'You do not find it slightly ludicrous to ask me such a personal question at the same

answering the query. 'I do not see why not. They are cousins by marriage, after all.'

'Yes, but—'

'I am still unsure as to whether—'

'You were rather abrupt with Braxton just now, Royston,' the dowager duchess cut off her friends' continued concerns as she turned to look at her grandson.

'Was I?' the duke returned unconcernedly.

'You know very well that you were.' His grandmother frowned.

'I am sure he will recover all too soon,' he murmured distractedly as he reached out to pierce another piece of fruit before holding it temptingly in front of Ellie.

Something Ellie—even in her 'naivety and inexperience'—knew to be entirely inappropriate. Nor did she care for the piercing intensity of Justin's glittering gaze at it rested on her parted lips.

At the same time she realised that *this* was what had changed so suddenly between them just minutes ago; one moment Justin had been berating her for her 'flirtatiousness' in what he believed to be her encouragement of Lord Caulfield and the next he had been shamelessly flirting with her himself. Just what was he up to?

Was this perhaps another lesson, to see if she had learnt anything from their conversation just now?

Whatever the reason for his behaviour, it had resulted in his drawing unwarranted attention to the two of them. As Ellie glanced nervously about them, she could see several of the older matrons in the near vicinity looking positively shocked at the intimacy of his

Chapter Seven

Madness.

Absolute bloody madness!

For there could be no other reason why Justin gave every appearance of behaving like a besotted fool, enticing his ladylove with succulent titbits of fruit.

Justin considered himself to be neither besotted nor a fool, Eleanor Rosewood was most certainly not his ladylove—nor would she ever be—and the only enticing that had ever interested him, where any woman was concerned, took place between silken sheets—and it was fruit of the forbidden kind!

He looked into those emerald-green eyes just inches from his own and knew from the uncertainty, the slight panic he detected in their depths, that Eleanor's casual dismissal just now was purely an act she had assumed for their audience. That the widening of her pupils, the bloom of colour in her cheeks, her slightly parted lips, and the barest movement of her breasts as she breathed shallowly, were indicative of what she was really feeling.

back of his chair. 'How can it be anything else when we all know I have no romantic intentions whatsoever where Eleanor is concerned.'

'I really must thank you for your most recent lesson, your Grace.' Ellie had heard quite enough of 'the Duke of Royston's' opinions for one evening. Arrogant, mocking, insufferable gentleman that he was!

Unfortunately, she also found him verbally challenging, dangerously handsome and physically exciting, to the extent that she suspected she might still be in love with him, despite previous private denials to the contrary.

Just to look at this man, to be in his company, to exchange verbal swords with him, still, in spite of her inner remonstrations with herself, caused her heart to beat faster, her breathing to falter and every nerve ending in her body to become thrillingly aware of everything about him. And Ellie knew she had almost succumbed to his dangerous allure as he had held that sliver of pineapple up in front of her so temptingly.

It had been so intimate an act, the noise and chatter about them seeming to disappear as the world narrowed down to just the two of them, and Ellie had found herself totally unable to look away from those piercing sapphire-blue eyes.

Much, she realised now, like a butterfly stuck on the end of a pin by its curious captor!

Certainly his next comment had shown that he had felt none of the physical awareness of her that she now had of him. Indeed, he had merely confirmed what

with indignation, at his highhandedness, for the whole of that time!

She removed her hand from his arm the moment they were outside in the less crowded Great Hall. 'How dare you! Who are you to embarrass me in front of other people, by questioning whether or not I might have behaved so scandalously as to have arranged to meet Lord Caulfield privately?'

Justin eyed her calmly, knowing himself to be once again in control—thankfully—of this situation. And himself. For he had not been as immune to Eleanor's physical awareness of him just now, when he'd attempted to feed her the pineapple, as he had given the impression of being…

No, indeed, he had risen to the occasion in spite of himself and had been forced to remain seated at the table for several minutes longer than necessary in order to wait until the bulge in his breeches became less obvious.

Much to his increasing annoyance.

Eleanor Rosewood's role as a protégée of his grandmother's, and his own ward, now rendered her as being completely unsuited to ever becoming his mistress. Nor did she meet the stringent requirements of a prospective duchess. As such there was no place for her in his well-ordered life, other than the annoyance of being forced by circumstance into acting as her guardian. All was not lost, of course; any number of women here this evening could, and in the past had, assuaged his physical needs.

'Who am I?' Justin repeated in a suddenly steely

Ellie's throat moved as she swallowed nervously, once again aware of the sudden tension that had sprung up between them, of how the very air that surrounded them now seemed charged with—with she knew not what.

The only thing she was sure of was the fluttering of excitement beneath her breasts, of the dampness to her palms inside her lace gloves, of the burn of colour blooming in her cheeks as his eyes continued to glitter down at her.

She swallowed again before speaking. 'I do not believe that is what I was doing.'

'No?'

'No,' she said defiantly.

A nerve pulsed in his tightly clenched jaw. 'I disagree.'

'That is your prerogative, of course—what are you doing?' she squeaked as the duke took a firm grasp of her arm before pulling her down the shadowed hallway, away from the crowded public salons, to where the private family rooms were situated. 'Justin?' she prompted sharply as he threw open the library door and pushed her unceremoniously inside the darkened room.

He followed her inside before closing the door firmly behind him. 'Of all the times I have asked you to do so, you must choose now to decide to call me Justin?' He towered over her in the darkness. 'I do believe you are challenging me, after all, Eleanor,' he murmured huskily.

It took Ellie several moments to adjust her eyes to

fuller, firmer, the tips tingling with an almost painful ache, an inexplicable dampness between her thighs, the whole experience making her legs feel weak.

As clear evidence that she did indeed love this man…

The warmth of his breath brushed softly, sweetly, against her temple as he bent his head closer to her own before murmuring, 'Little girls who deliberately wake the tiger deserve to be…punished, just a little, do you not think?'

Ellie quivered in awareness, felt as if his close proximity had sucked all the air from the room, her head beginning to whirl as she tried to breathe, and failed. 'Please…!' she gasped at the same time as she lifted her hands to his chest with the intention of pushing him away, of allowing her to draw in a breath. Only to find she had no strength left to do so, that instead of pushing him away her hands lingered, as if with a will of their own, her fingers splaying almost caressingly against the heat of his broad chest.

'Please what, Eleanor?'

'I—' She moistened lips that had become suddenly dry. 'I should go…'

'You should, yes.' He nodded slowly as he moved even closer, so that the silk of her gown and his own clothing were all that now separated them. 'The question is, are you going to do so?'

She looked up at him searchingly, the shadows cast by the moonlight making it impossible for her to read the expression on the male face only inches above her own. Even so, she could see enough to know the duke's

room with Eleanor, but he should certainly have kept his distance from her, and definitely not given in to the temptation to feel her slender curves so soft and sensuous against his much harder ones.

He could not even put his rashness down to an over-indulgence in brandy this evening, either, having been watching Eleanor so intently, as she danced with what seemed like a legion of other gentlemen, that there had not been the time to allow a single drop of the restorative liquid to pass his lips.

No, it was Eleanor herself who had intoxicated him this evening. Whose every word challenged him. Who had aroused him earlier, causing him to swell and throb inside his breeches, just by watching her lick the juice of the pineapple from the swell of her lips, until Justin had desired, hungered, for the sweet taste of those lips for himself. As he still hungered.

'Well, does it feel like a game?' he repeated as she didn't answer.

Her little pink tongue moved moistly across her lips before she finally responded in a breathy voice. 'Not any game I have ever played before, no.'

'Good.' Justin gave a hard, satisfied smile. 'And would you like to know what happens next in this particular…game?'

'Your Grace—'

'Justin, damn it!' He glared down at her, watching her face as he pressed his thighs against her, only to give a low and aching groan in his throat as pleasure immediately shot hotly down the length of his arousal.

had known that she could never be intimate in that way with a man she did not love and who did not love her, either. It was too personal, too carnal, too—too wild, for her to ever contemplate such personal intimacy taking place with a man whom she merely *liked.*

Justin's expression softened slightly as he obviously now saw, or perhaps sensed, her uncertainty. 'You do not believe me?'

'I—I do not know what to think, or say…' A slow shake of her head accompanied the hesitancy of that denial.

He grinned. 'Well, that is certainly a novelty in itself!'

'You are laughing at me again.'

Justin sobered, glittering gaze fixed intensely on the pale oval of her face. 'What would you like me to do with you?'

She caught her bottom lip between small pearly white teeth, nibbling that tender flesh for several seconds before her chin rose in challenge. 'I believe I should like for you not to treat me as a child.'

He smiled. 'Oh, I assure you, Eleanor, at this moment you are far from appearing as a child to me.'

She nodded. 'Then you will please tell me what happens next in this game?'

Justin drew in a sharp breath. 'Usually the gentleman now nuzzles his lips against the lady's throat. Like this.' He suited his actions to his words, enjoying her perfumed and silky skin against his lips.

The thrill of the sensations currently coursing through her body were so completely new to her, felt so strange, but not unpleasant, a mixture of both a shivery and hungry ache, and heated pleasure.

'Hmm, then perhaps we should continue until you do know.' Justin nibbled deliciously on the swollen flesh above her gown, his hips arched into hers as he continued that slow and leisurely thrusting.

And each time he did so Ellie felt that same pleasure, that swelling and moistness between her thighs becoming more intense as she now moved restlessly against him, seeking, wanting, oh God, aching for she knew not what…!

Her hands reached up to grasp tightly on to those impossibly wide shoulders, steadying her, anchoring her, even as she arched her thighs up to meet his thrusts, her breath now coming in short, strangled gasps. 'Please! Oh, Justin, please do not torture me any longer!'

Justin drew back slightly as he heard the anguish in her voice, knowing by the glazed look in her eyes, the flush to her cheeks, that she was close, so very close to orgasm. An orgasm, that in her innocence, she was completely unprepared for.

An innocence which he had been seriously in danger of shattering!

It took every effort of will he possessed to place his hands on her shoulders and pull away from her, feeling like the bastard he undoubtedly was as he saw the bewilderment in her expression. 'And it is for this reason,

Chapter Eight

Ellie blinked dazedly, wrapping her arms about herself as she felt suddenly cold, bereft, now that the heat of Justin's body had been withdrawn from her, that chill entering her veins, and then her heart, as she saw the expression on his arrogantly disdainful face, and realised that the past few minutes had been all about teaching her yet another of those 'lessons' in how to *not* behave in society.

Physically roused he might have been, but it had been a controlled and deliberate arousal on his part, and obviously nothing like the unbelievable pleasure Ellie had experienced when he had kissed and caressed her. No doubt even the proof of his arousal had been deliberate on his part, as a way of showing her just how little she really knew about men, and the weakness of her own body in responding to them, while he seemed to have put the whole incident behind him as if totally unmoved by it.

Her arms dropped back to her sides as she drew her-

Eleanor paused to turn in the hallway. 'I trust I may safely assume that you have no more "lessons" for me this evening, your Grace?'

'You may,' he confirmed, having already decided that he had attended his grandmother's ball for quite long enough. Far too long, in fact, when he considered how close he had been, just minutes ago, to making passionate love to Eleanor Rosewood in his grandmother's library!

Nor was that passion completely dampened even now, this distant, haughty Eleanor equally, if not even more challenging, than the defiant one of a few minutes ago. But it was a challenge Justin could not, dared not, allow himself to take up. Even if the uncomfortable throbbing of his unappeased shaft might demand otherwise.

As he already knew, there was an easy solution to that last problem. Instead of seeking one of the women here tonight, he would go to one of the houses of the *demi-monde,* settle on one of the pretty and willing woman to be found there and satisfy those demands in that way. Without expectation on either side. More importantly, without complication.

For it was quickly becoming obvious to Justin that his desire for Eleanor could become—indeed, if it was not already—a serious complication in his life.

'Royston?'

Justin, having already instructed Stanhope to bring his cloak and hat, with the intention of leaving Royston

aged widower wishing to court her. 'I believe you are referring to my ward, Miss Eleanor Rosewood?'

'Just so.' Richmond ran an agitated hand through his prematurely white hair. 'I—would it be impertinent of me to enquire as to her exact age?'

'It would, yes.' Surely Eleanor was too young for him?

The earl's eyes widened as he realised what his question had sounded like to Justin. 'No, no, Royston, it is nothing like that. Miss Rosewood is far too young for my interest,' he assured hastily. 'I just—if not her age, would it be possible for you to tell me who her mother is?'

'Was,' Justin corrected guardedly, having absolutely no idea, now that Richmond had assured him so positively he had no marital intentions towards Eleanor, what this conversation was about. But he felt sure, from the intensity of the earl's mood, that it was something which would further add to the complication Eleanor had already become in his life. 'Eleanor's mother was married to my cousin Frederick and, if you recall, he and his wife were both killed in a carriage accident just over a year ago.'

The earl gave a thoughtful frown. 'Frederick's wife was previously Muriel Rosewood…?'

'I believe I have just said so.'

'I had no idea… Of course, I have not been much in society for many years, and but even so I had not realised—' He broke off with a shake of his prematurely white head.

Justin looked taken aback. 'Now see here, Richmond, I do not—'

'Tell me, have you seen or heard any more of Litchfield?'

Justin's patience, never his strongest quality at the best of times—and this evening could certainly not be called that!—was almost non-existent as Richmond's conversation became even more obscure. 'As it happens we met him quite by accident whilst we were out riding in the park earlier today.'

'We? Miss Rosewood was with you?' the earl asked anxiously.

'What on earth does it matter whether Eleanor was with me or not?' Justin snapped.

'Everything! Or perhaps nothing,' the earl said vaguely. 'Did—is Litchfield now acquainted with Miss Rosewood?'

'I did not feel inclined to introduce the two of them, if that is what you are asking!'

Richmond sighed his relief. 'That is something, at least.'

'What does Eleanor riding with me earlier today have to do with the unpleasantness which exists between myself and Litchfield?'

'I shall not know the answer to that until we have spoken together tomorrow.'

Justin's previous interest in spending a passion-filled night with a willing woman was now fading as quickly as his patience. 'You are being very mysterious, Richmond.'

Litchfield? Whatever it was Justin now felt almost as unsettled as Richmond so obviously was.

Perhaps he should not have delayed the conversation until tomorrow, after all? It had been sheer bloody-mindedness on his part that he had done so in the first place; being guardian to Eleanor had already caused enough chaos in his life for one week—good God, had it really only been four days since his grandmother had made that ridiculous request of him?—and, as such, Justin had been unwilling to allow her to disrupt the rest of his plans for this evening.

'Where to, your Grace?' his groom prompted as he stepped forwards to open the door of the ducal carriage.

Justin ducked his head as he stepped up and inside. 'Curzon Street,' he said wearily as he sank back into the plush upholstered seat. 'You may take me home to Curzon Street, Bilsbury.'

Justin could see little point now in going on somewhere, or even in attempting to rouse his enthusiasm for any other woman, when his conversation with Richmond just now had succeeded in deflating any last vestiges of interest his libido might have had in partaking in such an exercise.

Damn his grandmother and her infernal interference.

Damn Richmond.

But, most of all, damn the irritating thorn Eleanor Rosewood had become in his side.

'It is such a beautiful day, ideal for a drive in the park!' Ellie smiled her pleasure at the outing as she

Ellie smiled as she realised she was being teased. 'I am sure that you did. It is only—I have never received so much as a single bunch of freshly picked spring flowers from a gentleman before, let alone so many beautiful displays.' The dowager duchess's private parlour was awash with the vases of flowers that had been delivered throughout the day, following the Royston Ball the evening before. Half a dozen of them were for the dowager duchess herself, of course, sent by other society matrons, as acknowledgement of the success of the ball, but the other dozen or so were for Ellie alone.

Notably, she had not received so much as a single blossom from the Duke of Royston. Oh, no, that toplofty gentleman would never deign to send a woman flowers, not even to his ward as a mark of the success of her introduction into society.

'I was only teasing, child.' Edith smiled across at her encouragingly. 'I could not be more pleased at your obvious success.'

Ellie forced the smile back to her lips. 'And you are not too tired from the ball and your late night?' Doctor Franklyn had been called to attend the dowager duchess this morning, but once again Ellie had been excluded from the bedchamber. Although she had not seemed to be too fatigued when she had joined Ellie for lunch in the small, family dining room earlier—it had been Edith's suggestion that the two of them go out for a carriage ride this afternoon.

Nevertheless, keeping true to her promise to Justin, Ellie had sent a short, formal note round to his rooms

was no longer even in the house, let alone the ballroom, had seemed to turn the evening flat, without purpose. Although what purpose a ball was supposed to have, other than dancing and flirtation, in which Ellie had engaged fully after Justin's departure, she had no idea!

She had fared no better, once the last guest had departed from Royston House and she was at last able to escape up the stairs to her bedchamber, her pillow seeming too lumpy for her to find any comfort, the covers either too hot or too cold. Unable to sleep, Ellie had not been able to prevent her thoughts from drifting to the time she had spent in the library with Justin.

Privately she could admit that it had been the most thrilling, the most physically sensuous, experience of her life. Of course, that might be because the only sensuous experiences of her life had been with Justin, rather than a confirmation of any softer emotions she might feel towards him.

There was some comfort to be found in that, she supposed. She had nothing, no other gentleman, with whom to compare her responses to Justin St Just. Perhaps any man turned a lady's legs to water when he kissed her and made her heart beat faster, caused her breasts to tingle and between her thighs to dampen? Ellie could only hope that might be the case.

'I doubt Royston will stir himself,' the dowager duchess answered Ellie's query dismissively. 'No doubt he will have gone on somewhere after he left us last night and will not have seen his bed until the early hours of this morning!'

Dryden Litchfield bared those brown-stained teeth in a smile. 'Royston introduced us yesterday.'

Ellie gasped softly at the blatant lie; the duke had not even attempted to introduce the two of them—indeed, Ellie believed Justin had gone out of his way not to do so. For just such a reason as this, no doubt; without the benefit of a formal introduction, Lord Litchfield should not have approached or spoken to her at all.

'Indeed?' The dowager gave Ellie a long and considering glance before that gaze became icier still as she turned back to Dryden Litchfield. 'You must excuse us, Lord Litchfield, I am afraid Miss Rosewood and I have another engagement which we must attend.' She nodded to him dismissively.

'But of course,' he drawled with feigned graciousness. 'Perhaps I might be allowed to call upon Miss Rosewood at Royston House…?'

Ellie gave another soft gasp, this time clearly of dismay, and Edith's mouth thinned disapprovingly at the man's bad manners. 'I do not think—'

'Miss Rosewood's time is fully engaged for the next week, at least.' A steely cold voice, easily recognisable to them all as Justin's, cut firmly across his grandmother's reply.

Ellie looked at him, only to shrink back against the carriage seat as those icily contemptuous blue eyes glanced briefly in her direction before returning to Litchfield.

'Then perhaps the week following that?' the other man persisted challengingly.

Ellie was wondering the same thing. Surely he did not seriously imagine for one moment that she had encouraged Lord Litchfield in any way?

A single glance beneath lowered lashes at the duke's cold blue eyes, thinned lips and tightly clenched jaw, showed her that he was, to all intents and purposes, furious.

Was he furious with her? And if so, why?

The drive back to Royston House was completed in silence, but Ellie was only too aware of the duke's continued anger as he rode beside the carriage on his magnificent black hunter, the expression on his face daring any in society to approach or speak to them. Wisely, none did.

Why Ellie should continue to feel quite so much as if that anger was directed personally at her was beyond understanding; despite what the duke might think, she had done nothing to encourage Lord Litchfield.

And yet still she felt as if all of the seething emotions she sensed behind Justin's stony façade were directed at her: anger, irritation and, for some inexplicable reason, resentment.

Quite why he should resent her was a mystery. If anyone should be feeling *that* particular emotion, then it should be Ellie herself, for she was the one who had once again been made a fool of the evening before, with her undeniable responses to this impossible man. Yes, indeed, all of the resentment should be on her side, not his!

been alone with her since their strained parting of the evening before. And yet it seemed as if days had passed since that time instead of hours, so much had transpired.

Usually Justin had no trouble sleeping, but he had found it impossible to fall into slumber the night before, physically frustrated of course, which was never a good thing, but also angry with himself for having kissed Eleanor yet again, and more than a little troubled as to what Richmond wished to discuss with him.

But he would never have guessed, could never have envisaged the full horror of the things Richmond had related to him earlier this afternoon.

Justin could not help but frown now as he looked down at Eleanor's bent head, her innocent head, and wonder how, if Richmond's suspicions should turn out to be correct, he would ever be able to tell her the truth, without utterly destroying the spirit in her that he so admired, as much as the fragile hold she now had in society.

No doubt Eleanor, never having needed that society before, would dismiss the importance of it in her life now, but Justin found he could not bear the thought of her independence of spirit also being trampled underfoot, snuffing out that light of either challenge or mischief he so often detected in her unwavering green gaze during their lively exchanges.

No, he would not tell Eleanor anything of that conversation as yet, preferring to make his own private and discreet enquiries, at least going some way towards proving—or disproving—Richmond's fears, before so

Chapter Nine

Ellie was painfully aware of Justin's sinfully handsome appearance as he stood beside her in a perfectly tailored superfine of sapphire blue, setting off buff-coloured pantaloons and brown-topped Hessians. There was an awkward silence between them, forcing her into making some sort of conversation.

She lifted her chin even as she tilted her head back in order to look up at him, feeling the physical discomfort at her nape in having to do so. 'Goodness, you are prodigiously tall!'

Blue eyes, the exact same shade as his superfine, widened briefly, before those chiselled lips twisted into a rueful smile. 'And you, brat, are incredibly rude, that you can never address a gentleman in the normal fashion of a well-bred young lady!'

'Perhaps I have been keeping company with you for too long?' she came back pertly.

'Perhaps you have,' he allowed. 'Shall we?' He held out his arm to her. 'Unless you wish to put my grand-

proval, 'it leaves me with no choice but to try to elicit the opinion on the subject from the one person who is with her the most.'

In truth, with all the excitement of the flowers arriving constantly throughout the day, the ride in the park, the encounter with the disagreeable Lord Litchfield, and then Justin's unexpected arrival a short time ago, Ellie had all but forgotten the note she had sent him following Dr Franklyn's visit.

Although Ellie could not help but admit to a certain grudging admiration for Dr Franklyn, in that he was insistent upon protecting his patient's confidentiality… much to the duke's obvious annoyance. She gave an inward smile.

'I believe her to be quite well, considering she was hostess to a ball yesterday evening, and the late hour at which we finally retired for the night,' Ellie said. 'Perhaps the doctor's visit was simply a precautionary one rather than a necessity?'

Justin pursed his lips. 'Perhaps.'

But, in Ellie's opinion, he did not sound at all certain. 'The dowager duchess did breakfast in her rooms, which is not her usual custom. But she did join me not long after that and we ate luncheon together. And it was her suggestion that we should ride in the park this afternoon.'

Justin's expression turned grim as he recalled who had been there with them when he had finally found Eleanor and his grandmother in the park earlier. 'I be-

straightened. 'I believe you are determined to misunderstand me—'

'Is that you at last, Royston, Eleanor?' his grandmother, obviously having heard the sound of their voices outside in the hallway, now called out impatiently.

Justin bit back his own impatience at this interruption as he lowered his voice so that only Eleanor might hear him. 'We will talk of this again later.'

'No, your Grace, I do not believe we will,' she snapped back, and obviously tired of waiting for him to open the parlour door for her, opened it for herself and preceded him into the room.

'Do not believe you will what, my dear?' the dowager enquired.

Justin followed Eleanor into the room. 'Will not—Good God, it is like a florist's shop in here!' He almost recoiled from the overabundance of perfume given off by the multitude of flowers in the room, vases and vases of them, it seemed, on every available surface. 'How on earth can you possibly breathe in here, Grandmama?' He strode across the room to throw open a window before turning to glare across at Eleanor. 'I suppose we have your success last night to thank for this gratuitous display?'

'Royston!' his grandmother rebuked sharply.

Justin' continued to glare at Eleanor. 'I am only stating the obvious, Grandmama!'

'That is no excuse for upsetting Ellie.' The dowager duchess rose to her feet to cross to Eleanor's side and place an arm about her shoulders. 'I am sure Royston

challengingly as she straightened out of the dowager's embrace, her chin held proudly high, sparks of anger in her eyes now rather than tears as she glared across at him. 'If you will both excuse me, I believe I will go to my room and tidy my appearance before dinner.' She sketched a brief curtsy before leaving the parlour with a swish of her skirts.

'Royston, what on earth was that all about?'

Justin closed his eyes momentarily before opening them again to look across at his grandmother, sighing deeply as he saw the reproach in her steely blue gaze. 'You no doubt wish for me to go to Eleanor and apologise for my churlishness?'

The dowager gave him a searching glance before replying. 'Only if that is what you wish to do yourself.'

Did he? Dare he follow Eleanor to her bedchamber? Allow himself to be in a position, a place, where he might be tempted into kissing her, making love to her once again?

'Obviously not,' his grandmother said acidly at his lengthy silence. 'Ah, Stanhope.' She turned to greet the butler warmly as he arrived with the brandy and tea. 'Wait a moment, if you please, and take this cup of tea to Miss Rosewood in her bedchamber.' She bent to pour the brew into the two delicate china teacups.

Justin was still fighting an inner battle with himself, aware that he had been overly sharp with Eleanor just now, and that he did owe her an apology for his behaviour, if not an explanation. For he had no intention of admitting to anyone, not even himself—least of all

His answer to that was to step further into the room and close the door behind him. 'I have brought you a cup of tea,' he repeated. 'And I will bring it across to you if you promise not to throw it over me the moment I place it in your hand!' he teased gently.

Ellie replaced the handkerchief in her pocket. 'You are an exceedingly cruel man.'

'Yes.'

'An insufferable man.'

'Yes.'

She frowned. 'Hateful, even.'

'Yes.'

Ellie blinked at his unexpected acquiescence to her accusations. 'Why do you not defend yourself?'

He sighed deeply. 'Possibly because, on this occasion, I know you are correct. I am all of the things you have accused me of being.'

Ellie eyed him guardedly, looking for signs of that sarcasm or cynicism she had also accused him of to herself just minutes ago. He met her gaze unblinkingly, the expression in those blue eyes neither cynical nor sarcastic, but merely accepting. 'I do not understand…'

'I am merely agreeing with you, Eleanor.' He crossed the room until he stood before her, the delicacy of the saucer and teacup he held out to her looking slightly incongruous in his lean hand.

She reached up slowly and took the cup and saucer from him. 'That is what I do not understand.'

He looked down at her beneath hooded lids as he gave a shrug of those broad shoulders. 'I have no de-

good as another gentleman having got down upon his knees and begged her forgiveness.

She placed the empty teacup and its saucer on the bedside table. 'Thank you. I do feel slightly better now.'

'Good.' He moved to sit on the side of the bed beside her and took one of her hands in both of his much larger ones. 'And I do sincerely apologise for my bad temper to you just now, Eleanor.'

Ellie, already disconcerted at the touch of his hands on hers, now looked at him in surprise. 'You do?'

He nodded. 'I was boorish, to say the least. I was a little…unsettled after seeing Litchfield, of all people, beside my grandmother's carriage in the park. But I accept I should not have taken that bad temper out on you.'

Ellie's heart had begun to beat faster at his sudden proximity, her cheeks feeling warm, her breathing shallow, and he surely must be able to feel the way her hand trembled slightly inside his? 'I really do not think it quite proper for you to be in my bedchamber. The dowager duchess—'

'Made it plain to me just now that she, at least, considers me to be nothing more than an uncle to you and, as such, feels it is perfectly permissible for me to visit you here,' he revealed drily.

The utterly disgusted expression on his face that accompanied this revelation only made Ellie feel like laughing again. How strange, when just minutes ago she had felt as if she might never laugh again…

Justin was completely unprepared for the way in which Eleanor's lips now twitched with obvious hu-

standing stiffly in front of the window. 'Who made these scurrilous remarks?'

She looked puzzled. 'I am not sure that I remember who exactly…'

A nerve pulsed in his tightly clenched jaw. 'Try!'

She gave a slow shake of her head. 'The remarks were not made to me directly, I merely overheard several people speculating as to who your current mistress might be, and which husband was being made the cuckold last night.'

'I assure you—' Justin broke off, realising he was angry once again, but this time at remarks made in Eleanor's hearing as to what society thought of him—a reputation which had not bothered him in the slightest until he had heard it from her lips… 'I wish you to know that I have the deepest respect for the married state, and as such have never shown the slightest inclination to bed a married woman. Nor,' he continued grimly, 'do I have a "current mistress".'

Ellie could tell by his expression that by repeating such gossip she had somehow succeeded in seriously insulting him. 'I did not mean to give offence, your Grace.'

'I am not in the least offended,' he denied.

'I beg to differ…'

His expression softened slightly. 'I am not offended by anything you have personally said to or about me, my displeasure is for those people who obviously have nothing better to do with their time than make up scan-

you to rejoin her in her parlour?' She linked her gloved hands tightly together in front of her. 'I really do have to change before dinner.'

'You have not said yet whether or not you believe my denials.'

She shrugged. 'Does it matter whether or not I believe you?'

Justin narrowed his lids as he noted the challenging tilt of her chin and the directness of her unreadable gaze.

He also realised that his own mood just now had been a defensive one. A feeling which was surely totally misplaced; it should not matter to him what his young ward thought of him, or his reputation. 'Not in the least,' he finally drawled.

Her gaze dropped from his. 'As I thought.'

Justin gave her a terse bow before striding across to the doorway. 'I will see you at dinner.'

'What?'

He paused to turn, his hand already on the door handle. 'I said we will meet again at dinner.'

She blinked. 'I had not realised her Grace had invited you to dine here this evening.'

Justin smiled. 'Of course...you were not present just now during the last part of my conversation with my grandmother.' He stood with his arms folded across his chest. 'If you had been, then you would know that it is my intention to dine here every evening for the foreseeable future. Breakfast, too, on the mornings I rise early enough to partake of it. I may be absent for the

Chapter Ten

'Why are you so surprised by my decision, Eleanor?' Justin asked as Ellie could only stare wide-eyed and open-mouthed across the bedchamber at him in the wake of his announcement. 'After all, you are responsible for alerting me to the fact that Dr Franklyn made yet another visit to my grandmother this morning.'

That might be so, but she certainly had not thought it would result in his decision to move into Royston House!

No doubt the dowager duchess was beside herself with pleasure at this unexpected turn of events, but it was equally as unthinkable to Ellie that she would have to suffer this disturbing man's presence every hour of every day 'for the foreseeable future'!

She moistened suddenly dry lips. 'Well, yes, I did do that, of course. But I did not mean it to—I had not expected—'

'You did not envisage it would result in your now having to suffer my living here?' Royston guessed drily.

change of heart, she would most assuredly question as to why it should have occurred now, of all times.

Ellie had dashed off that note to Royston this morning for the simple reason he had asked her to do so should such a thing occur, but she had not, as he so easily guessed and obviously found so amusing, expected to now have him thrust into her own life on a daily basis. Indeed, the very idea of it, given the circumstances of their own fraught relationship, was a total nightmare for her!

It was not too difficult for Justin to read the emotions flickering across her expressive face.

It was the last emotion—horror at the prospect of living with him—which irritated Justin the most. Especially when his real reason for moving into Royston House had everything to do with her, with the conversation that had taken place with Richmond this afternoon, and its possible repercussions upon Eleanor, rather than his grandmother's health, or any real desire on Justin's part to reside here.

It really was too insulting, given those circumstances, for him to have to suffer Eleanor's obvious dismay at the very thought of being under the same roof as him, of sharing even so large a residence as Royston House with him. But it was an insult he had no choice but to endure, unless he wished to tell her of the contents of his conversation with Richmond this afternoon, which, for the moment, he had no intention of doing.

Far better if Justin were to proceed with his previous decision to privately and quietly check into those

ish the sentence as he strode furiously across the room towards her.

Too late, Ellie realised her mistake in goading him, looking up just in time to see him powering towards her, fury blazing in those sapphire-blue eyes, causing her to step back even as she held her hands up defensively. 'Your Gr—er—Sir—Justin—'

'It's too late for that, Eleanor!' His arms moved about her waist as he pulled her in tightly against him, her hands trapped between the softness of her breasts and the muscled hardness of his chest. 'You are fully aware,' he grated, 'my feelings towards you are far from avuncular!'

How could she help but be aware of it when she could feel the evidence of his desire pressing into her abdomen!

Heat suffused her cheeks, her legs starting to tremble, as she looked at his face and saw evidence of that same desire blazing in the depths of the glittering blue eyes glaring down at her, high cheekbones thrown into sharp relief by the tight clenching of his jaw. 'You are crushing me, Your—Justin.' She turned her hands and began to push against the hardness of his chest in an unsuccessful attempt to free herself.

He bared his teeth in a humourless smile. 'And so now you learn, too late, my dear, the lesson that baiting the tiger is much worse than simply awakening him!'

She blinked. 'I was only—I merely—'

'I know exactly what you were doing, Eleanor—and *this* is my answer!' His head swooped downwards as he

tinued to kiss and caress her, moving restlessly against him as she dampened between her thighs, groaning low in her throat, as his knee moved up to press gently against that sensitive nubbin she had recently discovered nestled there, even as his thumb and fingers plucked rhythmically at her now hardened and oh-so-sensitive nipple.

He dragged his lips from hers to trail kisses hotly across her cheek and down her throat, his breath warm, arousing, against the heat of her flesh, that tingling in her breasts rising to fever pitch as his lips and tongue now tasted the swell visible above her gown and causing another rush of dampness between her thighs.

'Justin!' she cried out achingly as his hand left her breast.

'Yes—Justin,' he growled intensely, his hand sliding up her back. 'Say it, Eleanor. Say it, damn it!'

'Justin,' she breathed obediently. 'Oh God, Justin, Justin, Justin…!' That last trailed off to a groan as she felt his tongue laving the throbbing, engorged tip of her bared breast, having no idea how that had come about, only knowing that it gave her pleasure beyond imagining as he now took that hardened tip fully into the moist heat of his mouth.

Her fingers became entangled in the silkiness of his hair even as she arched up into that demanding mouth, sensations such as she had never known existed coursing through her as she felt his hand now cup her other bared breast, thumb and finger capturing the ripe tip,

The backs of her knees held the warmth of velvet, her thighs as smooth as silk, satin drawers posing no difficulty as Justin sought, and found, the slit in that material between her thighs, allowing his fingers to slip inside to gently stroke her swollen, wet folds.

He dipped his fingers into that moisture even as he heard Eleanor's gasp, half in shocked protest, half in pleasure, stroking her again and again, bathing his fingers in that moisture between each stroke, drawing her nipple deeply into his mouth in the same rhythm, until she no longer protested but groaned her pleasure as she writhed beneath him.

Justin was aware of the moment her hands fell down on to the bed beside her in surrender, of her head moving restlessly from side to side on the pillows, and he at last parted the silky folds and bared her sensitive and swollen nubbin to his caressing fingers and began to stroke in earnest. Softly and then harder, each time increasing the pressure, measuring his strokes to the rhythmic lifting of her hips, as she met each and every one of them, until he knew she was poised on the brink of a shattering release.

'Oh, it is too much…!' she gasped in protest, yet at the same time unable to stop herself from arching up into those caresses, her fingers once again entangled tightly in his hair as she held his mouth against her breast. 'Justin, do something…!'

Justin knew he was damned if he did. Damned if he did not. Because, he knew, whether he gave her the release she so obviously craved, or stopped this before that

Ellie had no idea how long it lasted, how many minutes, hours, had passed as she lost herself to that release as Justin demanded and took every last measure of that pleasure.

But finally, immeasurable minutes later, he gentled those stroking fingers between her thighs, softened his tongue against her now throbbing and aching breasts, placing one last lingering kiss against each swollen tip before he rolled to one side and moved up on his elbow to look down at her. 'I did not hurt you, did I?'

The gruffness of his voice was a thrill in itself as it wound itself sinuously along Ellie's already sensitive nerve-endings. Yet at the same time it broke the sensuous spell she had been under, allowing her to become aware of exactly what she had allowed to happen.

The Duke of Royston had just made love to her, touched her, more pleasurably, more intimately than any man had ever dared to attempt before now. More intimately than Ellie should have allowed any man to touch her before her wedding night!

Something that would never happen for her with the cynically arrogant Justin St Just, who wasn't interested in loving his bride or having those feelings returned. And she had probably just added to that cynicism and arrogance, with her easy capitulation to his seduction!

She scrambled up into a sitting position, blushing as she drew her legs up beneath her defensively, to clutch her gaping gown against her to cover her now painfully aching breasts. It allowed her to see that he was still fully and impeccably dressed, necktie still in place,

he had just said, knowing that she'd had no will to call a halt, no strength to resist his caresses. But he had. Oh, yes, the arrogant Duke of Royston had remained completely in control of his own senses, whilst her feelings for him meant that she had melted at his first touch. How humiliating. 'I told you to leave,' she repeated woodenly.

'Eleanor, listen to me, damn it!' He frowned down at her in frustration. 'If I had stopped you would now be berating me for leaving you in a state of dissatisfaction that would have clawed at you for hours, instead of which—'

'Instead of which I can now claim to have been the latest recipient of the irresistible Duke of Royston's expert lovemaking!' she threw back.

He drew in a sharp breath. 'I refuse to take offence at your insults. I realise that you are…upset.' He ran agitated hands through his hair, those golden waves instantly falling back into their artfully dishevelled style. As if he had made the gesture a hundred times before and knew its effect. After making love to a hundred different women, no doubt!

It infuriated Ellie all over again to know that she was nothing more to this man than another notch on his bedpost. 'Oh, by all means take offence,' she invited scathingly. 'For, I assure you, I am not so upset that I do not know exactly what I am saying when I warn you never to touch me ever again!'

'We will talk of this when you are calmer—'

'No, we will not,' she insisted firmly.

clenching into fists at his sides. 'Nor have we done anything this evening that in the least damages that innocence, or your reputation in society.'

She looked at him wordlessly for several long seconds before giving a slow shake of her head. 'I have little or no regard for my reputation in society, sir, but my innocence is certainly now questionable.'

'No—'

'Yes,' she hissed. 'You, of all people, must know that I had no idea—no knowledge of—' She stopped and gathered herself. 'My maidenhead may indeed still be intact, but my innocence is not.' Her cheeks were flushed. 'Now, would you please, please leave me.' Her voice finally wavered emotionally, the over-bright glitter in her eyes confirming that she was on the edge of tears.

Tears, which Justin knew with a certainty, she would not wish him to see fall. 'I trust you understand how impossible it is for me to even attempt to explain to my grandmother why I have changed my mind about moving into Royston House?'

Eleanor's shoulders straightened proudly. 'I understand. Just as I am sure that the two of us are adult enough, and both have enough affection for the dowager duchess, if not for each other, to do everything in our power to be polite to one another whenever we are in her company or that of others.'

Telling Justin, more surely than anything else could have done, that Eleanor had no intention of being in the least polite to him when they were alone…

your Grace, and I assure you, I will scream until all the household comes running!' Ellie warned him with icy pride; she might have allowed herself to be seduced by her feelings for this man, but that did not mean he would ever know of them.

He straightened, eyes glittering. 'This is far from over, Eleanor.'

'Oh, but it is,' she insisted. 'There will be no more "lessons" for me from you tonight. Or, indeed, any other night! Now please leave my bedchamber.' She turned her face away to indicate an end to the conversation, her heart pounding in her chest as she waited to see if Justin would do as she asked. Having no idea what she would do if he did not!

There was deathly silence for several minutes, then Ellie heard the opening of the door, before it was gently closed again seconds later.

At which time she allowed the tears to fall as she began to cry as if her heart were breaking.

Which it was.

out visiting, accompanied by her maid or the dowager. And, without Eleanor being aware of it, one of the footmen from Royston House, as extra protection from the threat Justin now considered Litchfield to be.

Not that Justin could blame Eleanor for that avoidance. No, despite that bump on his head from the blow of the saucer, and the headache that had followed, she was not the one to blame for the strain which now existed between them. The blame for that clearly lay entirely on Justin's own shoulders. He had fully deserved her anger, her physical retribution, had seriously overstepped a line with her. One Justin, even with his nine more years of maturity and experience, had absolutely no idea how to cross back over. Eleanor's frosty demeanour towards him certainly gave him the clear impression she had no wish for him to even try healing the breach between them!

Justin had spent the same three days trying to ascertain more about the events of twenty years ago, where Muriel Rosewood had gone to live once she returned to England, and what had become of her. Something which, without the help of Muriel herself, was not proving as easy as Justin had hoped it might. Many of the soldiers who had been in India at the same time as Litchfield, but later also returned to England, had died during the battles against Napoleon, and their widows, or the soldiers who had survived, were scattered all over England.

The Rosewood family had proved most unhelpful, too, the note of query Justin had delivered to their Lon-

to have disturbed your reverie, Royston.' He turned to leave.

'No! No, really, Thorne,' Justin repeated wearily as the other man turned to arch one dark, questioning brow. 'Please, do excuse my rudeness and join me, by all means.' He indicated the chair on the opposite side of the fireplace.

The same age as Justin, Adam Hawthorne had never been a particular friend of his until recently, despite their grandmothers' lifelong friendship. But the two men had been involved together in a matter personal to Hawthorne just weeks ago. One, which, thankfully, had been resolved in a manner most satisfactory to Hawthorne and the woman to whom he was now betrothed.

Justin waited until the other man was seated before speaking again. 'Was there something in particular you wished to discuss with me?'

'As it happens, yes.' Hawthorne, known in the past for his taciturn and prickly nature, hence the reasoning for that shortened version of his surname, now gave a boyish grin. 'You are aware, no doubt, of my upcoming nuptials…?'

'Oh, yes.' Justin rolled his eyes. It was the announcement of Hawthorne's betrothal, and forthcoming marriage, which had caused Edith to renew even more strongly her urgings that it was past time he chose a bride for himself.

Hawthorne gave a sympathetic smile. 'The dowager still proving difficult?'

him immensely if he were to learn that he had fallen victim to her wily machinations.

Except Justin knew he wasn't living with her solely out of concern for her health, that it was also concern for Eleanor—which she would likely not appreciate if she knew of it—that had been the main factor in his decision. He was only too well aware now of Litchfield's viciousness of nature, which in turn made Eleanor, and Justin's grandmother, both prime targets if the earl should decide to act upon that viciousness.

'Royston…?'

Justin gave himself a mental shake as he returned his attention to Hawthorne. 'You mentioned your upcoming nuptials…?'

The other man nodded. 'You have made quite an impression on my darling Magdelena, you know.'

'Indeed?' He eyed the other man warily; Miss Matthews was a beautiful and charming young woman, and he had been pleased to assist Hawthorne in freeing her of the devil who had been so determined to ruin her life, but other than that he had no personal interest in her, and if Hawthorne thought otherwise—

'So much so,' Hawthorne continued, 'that she will hear of nothing less than that you stand as one of the witnesses at our wedding.'

'Me?' Justin could not have been more shocked if Hawthorne had invited him to dance naked at Almack's!

Hawthorne's eyes gleamed with devilish laughter. 'I realise how unpleasant that task must be to one as opposed to matrimony as you are, but Magdelena is set

Which explained why Eleanor had been accompanying the dowager on her visits to Lady Cicely's home recently, as Miss Matthews was residing with Lady Cicely until after the wedding.

'Indeed,' Hawthorne continued, 'the two of them are out together now, in the company of our mutual grandmothers, deciding upon material for Magdelena's wedding gown.'

Damn it, it appeared that Hawthorne knew more about Eleanor's movements than he did! Which, given the circumstances of her complete aversion to his own company, was not so surprising...but was incredibly galling.

'My young daughter, Amanda, who is to be a bridesmaid, is also with them,' Hawthorne relaxed back in his chair. 'A great concession on her part, believe me, as she would much rather be in the stable with her pony than shopping for dresses. I believe it was her deep affection for Magdelena and Magdelena's for her—and, of course, the bribe of calling at Gunter's for ice-cream, once the unpleasant task has been completed—which went a long way towards convincing Amanda otherwise!'

So it seemed that Hawthorne's daughter from his first marriage had not been in the least excluded from her father's happiness in his forthcoming marriage. Or, quite obviously, the time and affections of her future stepmother.

Hawthorne quirked a questioning brow. 'Why are you looking at me so strangely?'

Justin's jaw tightened; he had not realised he was

'It would be considered a good match for your young ward,' Hawthorne continued conversationally, seemingly unaware of Justin's sudden turmoil of emotions. 'Endicott is both wealthy and second in line to a dukedom.'

Admittedly, Endicott was indeed as Hawthorne described, and at two and twenty, he was also considered charming and handsome by those society mamas looking for a suitable and wealthy son-in-law. But as far as Justin was aware Eleanor had only met the other man once, on the evening of the Royston Ball, when she stood up to dance a single set with him. Of course, he had noted that one of those dozens of bouquets of flowers, delivered the day after the ball, could have been sent from Endicott, but even so...

Justin gave a decisive shake of his head. 'I have no idea how you have hit upon such a misconception, Hawthorne, but I assure you that Eleanor does not have any such ambitions where Endicott is concerned.'

'Oh?' Hawthorne looked surprised. 'In that case, perhaps it might be kinder if she were to discourage his attentions, rather than appearing as if she enjoyed them.'

Justin looked confused. 'I have absolutely no idea what the devil you are talking about!'

The other man gave him a speculative glance before replying slowly, 'No, apparently you do not...'

'What do you think, Ellie?' Miss Magdelena Matthews prompted as their party stood outside Gunter's

back of the house—whilst the latter took over the study and library for the duke's personal use.

Edith St Just, as predicted, had been beside herself with joy at this turn of events. Indeed, the dowager had been flushed with excitement ever since, thankfully showing no sign of the illness or fatigue that had previously plagued her, as she happily reorganised the household to fit around the duke's daily schedule.

Ellie had been far from joyous. In fact, she had hoped, once Justin had time to consider the matter following the incident in her bedchamber, that he would have sensitivity enough to find a way in which to delay—indefinitely!—his plans to move in.

She should have realised that would be expecting too much from a man who obviously cared for nothing and no one, other than his grandmother's comfort and, of course, his own!

Ellie was therefore left with no choice but to absent herself from Royston House as much as possible. Something that had proved only too easy to do when the invitations, to theatre parties, dances and assemblies, and alfresco dining, had flooded in following her success at the Royston Ball. And, too, she had developed a deep friendship with Magdelena Matthews, the two of them finding they had much in common as they talked together whilst the dowager was visiting with her dear friend Lady Cicely.

Indeed, if not for Justin's depressingly broody presence at Royston House, and her unrequited love for

rée this evening?' he enquired eagerly. 'If so, might I be permitted to—?'

'My ward plans to spend this evening at home, Endicott,' a cold voice cut repressively across their conversation.

A voice Ellie recognised only too easily.

As indeed did the others in her group as they all turned in unison to look at him, the dowager with some surprise, Lady Cecil and Miss Matthews with some considerable curiosity.

Ellie took a moment to straighten her spine—and her resolve—before she also turned to look at him, instantly aware that neither her straightened spine or her resolve were sufficient for her to withstand the icy blast of his glittering blue gaze as it swept over her before alighting on the hapless Lord Charles Endicott, as that young gentleman bowed to the older man.

Lord Endicott was a picture of dandified elegance in his superfine of pale blue and waistcoat of pastel pink, the collar of his shirt uncomfortably high, neckcloth intricately tied at his throat, and giving him all the appearance of a posturing peacock when placed next to Justin's sartorial elegance, in grey superfine, charcoal-coloured waistcoat and snowy white linen.

Although possibly only half a dozen years separated the two men, they were as different as day and night, the one so bright and colourful, the other a study of dark shadows.

Ellie bristled defensively as she saw the contemptuous curl of the duke's top lip, and the scathing amuse-

which still coursed through her each and every time she thought of what they had done together!

Nevertheless, she did not welcome him bringing attention to her fatigue, or even in mentioning it at all! 'I have no intentions of cancelling attending Lady Littleton's soirée this evening.'

'Oh, I believe that you will,' the duke answered softly, dangerously, as their gazes remained locked, his challenging, Eleanor's defiant.

'No.'

'Yes!'

'Royston?' the dowager duchess prompted sharply at this public battle of wills.

It had not been Justin's intention to leave the carriage when he had instructed his driver to return to Royston House by way of Berkeley Square, but a single glance towards the establishment known as Gunter's had revealed Eleanor and his grandmother to be standing outside, in the company of the female members of Hawthorne's family.

And that blasted Endicott fellow!

Justin had not given himself time to think as he instructed his driver to stop, barely allowing his carriage to come to a halt before jumping out on to the cobbled road and marching towards where the happy group lingered in conversation.

Just in time, it would seem, to prevent Eleanor from making yet another assignation with Endicott, for later this evening!

'But what is your reason for denying Elli—Eleanor the pleasure of going to Lady Littleton's soirée this evening?'

It had been Justin's experience that such evenings were both tedious and tiresome, rather than a pleasure! 'As I have already stated, Grandmama—' he maintained a pleasant, reasoning tone '—Eleanor looks somewhat fatigued and I simply feel that an evening at home resting would be more beneficial to her health than another night out.'

'I—'

'You must forgive me, Eleanor, I had not noticed before now,' the dowager duchess spoke over Eleanor's angry protest, 'but Royston is right; you are indeed looking slightly pale and fatigued this afternoon.'

'There.' Justin turned to Eleanor, triumph glittering in his eyes. 'I do not believe the dowager and I can both be wrong?'

Ellie narrowed her eyes on her tormentor's gaze, dearly wishing that the two of them were alone at this moment—so that she might launch another cup and saucer at his arrogant head! Or a heavy tome. Or perhaps something even deadlier than that! For she did not believe a word of what he had just said, from his 'having just been passing by' in his carriage to his obviously fake concern about her supposed 'fatigue'.

Considering the size of the city, and the numerous other pursuits the duke could have been enjoying today, it seemed far too coincidental that he should have been 'driving past' Gunter's at this precise moment. Nor did

'Oh, I say—'

'Did you have something you wished to add to this conversation, Endicott?' Cold blue eyes focused with deadly intent on the younger man at his interruption.

Ellie could not help but feel sorry for Charles Endicott at that moment, his face first suffusing with embarrassed colour, and then as quickly paling, as Justin continued to glower down at him, appearing every inch the powerful and haughty Duke of Royston; it was like watching a fluffy little lapdog being confronted by a ferocious wolfhound. Indeed, Ellie would not have been in the least surprised if the duke's top lip had not curled back in a snarl to bare a long and pointed incisor at the younger man!

'Perhaps it would be as well if you were to return with Royston, Eleanor.' The dowager duchess, ever sensitive to not causing a scene in public—unlike her arrogant grandson!—agreed smoothly. 'I am perfectly happy to go alone to Lady Cicely's.'

Ellie was bursting with indignation at Justin's high-handedness, longing to tell him exactly what he could do with his offer to drive her home in his carriage—which had not been an offer at all but an instruction! At the same time she knew she could not, would not, do or say anything which might upset the dowager duchess; she owed that dear lady too much to ever wish to cause her embarrassment—the very clothes she stood up in, in fact!

'Then we are all agreed.' The duke took a firm hold of Ellie's arm. 'Ladies.' He bowed to them politely. 'En-

she had allowed herself to be put into his carriage, the door having already been closed to shut them inside.

It was the first time Ellie had been completely alone with him since—well, since 'that night', as she had taken to referring to it in her mind. And to her chagrin she was instantly, achingly aware, of everything about him. The golden sweep of his hair, the glitter of deep-blue eyes set in that hard and chiselled face, the way the superb cut of his superfine emphasised the width of his shoulders and tapered waist, his legs long and powerful in pale grey pantaloons and black Hessians.

Her feelings for him also made her aware of the tingle of sensations which now coursed through her own body, her breasts feeling achingly sensitive, that now familiar warmth between her thighs.

A reaction which only increased her growing anger towards him…

Justin did not need to look at Eleanor's face to know that she was furious with him; he could feel the heat of that anger as her eyes shot daggers across the short distance of the carriage that separated them.

Justifiably so, perhaps. He had behaved badly just now. Very badly. Towards both Eleanor and Endicott. A fact his grandmother would no doubt bring him to task over at her earliest opportunity.

And yet Justin did not regret his actions. Not for a moment. He had been incensed from the first moment he had seen that young dandy Endicott made up one of his grandmother's party. To add insult to injury, his

give my permission for you to marry that young peacock, you might just as well give it up now and cease your encouragement of him.'

'I was *not* encouraging him—'

'I beg to differ,' he cut in harshly. 'And it is not only I who appears to think so,' he continued as she would have made another protest. 'Indeed, the society gossips have it that there will be an announcement made before the end of the Season!'

Her eyes widened. 'I beg your pardon?'

Justin shrugged. 'The two of you are currently the talk of the *ton*.'

She gave another gasp. 'But I have only spoken to Lord Endicott on three occasions, once at the Royston Ball, again at a dinner party the evening before last, and then again at the park yesterday in the company of Miss Matthews.'

'And again just now,' he reminded her. 'That would appear to be four occasions in four days.'

'Well. Yes. But—I had no idea we would even be seeing Lord Endicott today!'

That was something, at least; Justin had been sure the two of them must have prearranged this latest meeting. 'I doubt Endicott's presence at Gunter's was as innocent as your own.'

A blush coloured her cheeks. 'He did mention something about having overheard Magdelena and I discussing the outing yesterday. Do *you* believe that Lord Endicott has serious intentions towards me?' she asked.

'Yes.'

appeared to either admire or fear the Duke of Royston. The ladies, married or otherwise, to desire him. The young débutantes considered him as being the catch of the Season—any Season this past ten years or so! The mothers of those débutantes appeared to either covet or avoid coming to his attention, aware as they were that the Duke of Royston had successfully avoided the parson's mousetrap for a long time; it would be a feather in any society matron's bonnet to acquire the Duke of Royston as her son-in-law, but equally it could be the social ruin of her daughter if he were to offer that young lady a liaison rather than marriage.

As such, Ellie had no idea who would have dared to make remarks about her to him. About herself and *Lord Endicott,* of all people. Why, she considered that young man as being nothing more than an amusing and playful puppy. Oh, he was handsome in a boyish way, and pleasant enough—if one ignored his atrocious taste in clothes—but her feelings for Royston meant she did not, and never would, consider Lord Endicott as being anything more than a friend. That anyone should ever imagine she might seriously consider *marrying* the foppish boy, was utterly ludicrous!

That Justin should believe such nonsense she found hurtful beyond belief. How could she possibly be interested in any other man, when Justin himself had ruined her for all others?

And Eleanor did not mean her reputation.

No, her ruination was much more fundamental than that, in that she simply could not imagine ever wishing

'But of course.' Her smile widened deliberately at his obvious astonishment. 'The dowager has informed me that a young lady can only really consider herself a complete success in society once she has broken at least half-a-dozen hearts and received and refused her third proposal!'

The duke's back straightened, his expression suddenly grim. 'I sincerely trust, just because of our recent interlude, you are not considering counting my own heart as among the ones which you have broken?'

Ellie forced an incredulous laugh to cover the jolt she felt at hearing Justin refer so dismissively to their lovemaking. 'I believe the only thing broken on that particular evening was a cup and saucer, your Grace. Besides,' she continued evenly, 'surely one has to be in possession of a heart for it to be broken?'

'So you do not believe I have one?'

She raised auburn brows. 'Are you not the one who once stated he has no intention of ever falling in love?'

His nostrils flared. 'I believe what I actually said was that I have no intention of being in love with my wife. But,' he continued drily as she would have spoken, 'you are actually correct. The truth is, I have no intention of falling in love with any woman.'

'Why not?' Ellie could have bitten out her tongue the moment she allowed her curiosity to get the better of her. And yet a single glance at his closed expression stopped her from instantly retracting the question.

But it *was* a curiosity that a man such as he, a man who could have any woman he wished for, had de-

turned to look out of the window beside her. 'I do not believe I may claim to have been particularly "prudent" in our…relationship, to date, your Grace.'

Justin could certainly vouch for that!

Indeed, Eleanor had been anything but prudent in her dealings with him this past week, to a degree that he now knew her body almost as intimately as he did his own: the satiny smoothness of her skin, the taste of her breasts, the warm touch of her lips and the expression on her face as she climaxed against his fingers.

Just as he could not help but notice the perfection of the calm profile she now turned away from him: the creamy intelligent brow, long lashes surrounding those emerald-green eyes, her cheek a perfect curve, freckle-covered nose small and straight, her lips full above her stubbornly determined chin.

Eleanor had grown in elegance as well as self-confidence this past week, her pale-green bonnet, the same shade as her gown, fastened about the pale oval of her face, with enticing auburn curls at her temples and nape, her spine perfectly straight, shoulders back, which only succeeding in pushing the fullness of her breasts up against the low bodice of her gown, knees primly together, dainty slippers of green satin peeping out from beneath the hem of her gown.

Yes, Eleanor was certainly the picture of an elegant and beautiful young lady, and Justin realised that her air of self-confidence was due to the admiration and attentions of fawning young dandies, of which Endicott was no doubt only one.

Chapter Thirteen

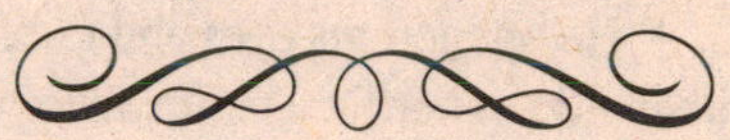

Justin rose and crossed to the other side of the carriage and sat down next to Eleanor, his thigh pressed against the warmth of hers. He reached out and pulled the curtains across each of the windows, throwing the interior of the carriage into shadow, but not dark enough for them not to be able to see each other and know what he was doing, as he untied the ribbon on Eleanor's bonnet before removing it completely.

'We will reach Royston House shortly…' she protested breathlessly.

Justin reached up and tapped on the roof of the carriage.

'Your Grace?' his groom responded.

'Continue to drive until I instruct you otherwise, Bilsbury.' Justin raised his voice so that he might be heard above the noise of the horses' hooves on the cobbled street.

'Yes, your Grace.'

Eleanor seemed frozen in place, unable to move or look away as Justin deftly removed the pins from those

She became totally lost in the barrage of emotions as he continued to kiss her. Then he lifted her above him, the length of her gown rising up her legs as she straddled his muscular thighs, allowing him to pull her in tightly against him, her knees resting on the seat either side of him.

Her drawers had parted, allowing the fullness of his arousal to press up against the swollen heart of her, only the material of his pantaloons now separating them.

Ellie gave a breathless gasp as the rocking of the carriage rubbed his firm length against the sensitive nubbin between her own thighs, totally lost to sensation as Justin unfastened the buttons at the back of her gown. He broke the kiss to ease her slightly away from him to allow her gown to drop away, revealing her breasts covered only by the thin material of her chemise, his eyes becoming hot and glittering as he raised his hands to cup the twin orbs.

Ellie looked down, her cheeks flaming as she saw what Justin had done; her breasts were fuller, the nipples swollen and hard at their tips as they pouted up and forwards invitingly.

'You are so beautiful…!' he murmured huskily, gently pushing her chemise aside before his head lowered to draw one of those swollen berries into his mouth.

Ellie's whole body now felt suffused with heat as she thrust her fingers into his hair, every caress of that moist tongue a torture that coursed hot and molten through her veins.

Ellie gave a relieved smile, capturing her tongue between her teeth in concentration as she unbuttoned his waistcoat and pulled up his shirt to bare his chest before allowing her gaze to become fixed once again on the hard, silken length of his shaft. She continued to caress him instinctively, fingers tightening around his arousal, responding to his groans of pleasure as she began to lightly pump up and down. Justin's thighs began to thrust up into the circle of her fingers and she tightened her grip as she heard his loud gasp, the expression on his face now almost one of pain, despite his earlier assurances.

Ellie stilled. 'I am sure I must be hurting you—'

'No!' He lifted his hand, fingers curling about hers as he encouraged her to continue that rhythmic pumping. 'Do not stop, Eleanor, please do not stop…!' His head dropped back against the upholstered seat, lids completely closed, long golden lashes dark shadows against the harsh planes of his sculptured cheeks.

Ellie had never seen anything as beautiful, as intensely wildly beautiful, as the fierceness of his pleasure in her caresses. It was somehow empowering, so fiercely primal, to know that she could give such pleasure to the man she loved.

'Harder,' he encouraged achingly. 'Oh lord, faster…!'

Ellie's fingers tightened further about him as she followed his instructions, eyes widening as his shaft seemed to grow even longer, thicker, with each downward stroke, the head more swollen, and glistening with moisture.

way in which she responded so willingly, so wantonly, to his every caress?

'Eleanor, *please?*' he begged at her continued silence.

It was unacceptable that this proud, powerful man should plead with her. That he should plead with anyone for anything!

Nor did she wish to continue to waste this precious time together lingering on her own emotions. 'Yes, I trust you, Justin,' she said, her hands clinging to the width of his shoulders as he sat up to edge forwards on the seat, his gaze once again holding hers captive as he began to move, the hardness of his shaft stroking against the swollen nubbin between her dampened thighs, the wetness there allowing his silken hardness to glide up and between her swollen folds rather than entering, breaching, the sheath beneath.

Ellie moaned in ecstasy as the nubbin between her thighs throbbed and pulsed in response to each stroke, her cheeks aflame with her arousal, her breathing ragged as she felt the pressure building inside her, taking her higher and ever higher, her breasts tingling almost painfully, as that heated pleasure between her thighs became almost too much to bear.

'Now, Eleanor!' Justin gasped between gritted teeth. 'I am going to—come for me now, Eleanor!'

His words meant nothing to Ellie, it was the tightening of his hands about her waist as he held her firmly in place, and the intensified throbbing and bucking of his shaft against her, that threw her totally over the

riage—a carriage that now reeked of the smell of sex! What on earth had he been *thinking?*

Ellie was so weakened, so lost in wonder, that it took her several minutes to realise that Justin's shoulder had tensed beneath her brow. His chest was steadily rising and falling against her breasts, while his hands had fallen away from her waist.

She raised her head warily and looked at his harshly etched features; there was a frown between his eyes, his cheekbones appeared like blades beneath the tautness of his skin, and his jaw was tightly clenched.

So clearly not the face of an indulgent and satiated lover.

She moistened her lips with the tip of her tongue before speaking. 'Are you angry with me?'

'With myself,' he corrected harshly.

Her eyes widened. 'Why?'

'You can ask me that?' He gave a self-disgusted shake of his head as he placed his hands on her waist once again in order to lift her off him and sit her on the seat beside him. He briskly pulled up the bodice of her gown and refastened the buttons at the back before straightening his own clothing.

Ellie's legs felt decidedly shaky as she pressed her knees tightly together, gasping as she felt another wave of pleasure emanate from that still-swollen nubbin nestled in the auburn curls between her thighs. Her cheeks suddenly blazed again as she became aware that the

* * *

Justin could not think of a single thing to say or do that would erase the expression of hurt bewilderment from Eleanor's face; that his behaviour had been reprehensible, totally beyond the pale, was beyond denial, as well as being a betrayal of his role as her guardian.

She still looked utterly dishevelled, delicate wisps of her hair having escaped her ministrations, her cheeks pale, her lips slightly swollen from the force of their kisses, her gown crushed and slightly soiled—and he winced just to think of the state of her underclothes.

Damn it, he had told himself after the first time that such a depth of intimacy must never happen between the two of them again. Nor did he believe it would have done so now, if he had not been so infuriated by her obvious enjoyment of Endicott's attentions, when recently she could barely spare him the time of day.

Which begged the question—why had Eleanor's obvious liking for Endicott so infuriated him, when the sooner she received a proposal of marriage from someone of Endicott's ilk, and accepted it, then the quicker Justin's own onerous responsibility as her guardian would come to an end? Just as her possible problematic connection to Litchfield would then become her husband's business rather than his own.

Which was exactly what Justin wanted, was it not? To be free of her so that he might return to his uncomplicated life before her come-out in society had caused him such inconvenience and irritation?

away from the hands he had lifted with the intention of lightly grasping her arms. 'Or be mistaken into thinking these tears are caused by anything other than anger, and a recognition of my own stupidity, in having once again having allowed myself to fall prey to your experienced seduction!'

Justin's jaw tightened grimly at the insult as he continued to look at her for several long seconds, aware of the challenge in her own gaze, before he drew in a deep breath and rose agilely to his feet to move and sit on the other side of the carriage. 'Better?'

Her chin rose as she replied just as tersely, 'Much.'

He let out a ragged sigh. 'Eleanor—'

'I really would prefer it if you did not speak to me again.' Her voice shook, whether with anger, or some other emotion, Justin was unsure. 'I have—I am in no fit state to talk about this now.' She gave a shake of her head, her gloved hands tightly clasped together in her lap.

Justin was surprised that either of them could speak at all after the intensity of their lovemaking! Indeed, his own body was currently filled with such lethargy, so physically satiated and drained, that he dearly longed for a hot bath in which he might ease away some of those aches and strains.

'Very well, Eleanor,' he acquiesced. 'But when you are feeling better—'

'I am not ill, your Grace,' she assured him with a humourless laugh. 'Merely full of self-disgust and recriminations,' she added honestly.

* * *

Ellie heaved a sigh of relief as she saw they were approaching Royston House at last, barely waiting for the carriage to come to a halt and the groom—Bilsbury, no doubt!—to open the door, before stepping quickly outside, in desperate need to put some distance between herself and Justin.

She would need to bathe and change her clothing, too, before Edith St Just arrived home; as Justin had already remarked, his grandmother was indeed a very astute lady, and the dowager would only need to take one look at Ellie's dishevelled appearance to realise exactly what must have taken place between them in Justin's carriage on their drive back to Royston House!

It was to be hoped that the dowager had not arrived home ahead of them…

Ellie had no idea how much time had passed while she and Justin made love in his carriage, but it would not have taken the dowager so very long to take tea with Lady Cicely. It would be too humiliating if she had arrived home ahead of them—

'We will go inside together, Eleanor.' The duke put his hand lightly beneath her elbow to fall into step beside her as she hurried up the wide steps fronting the house.

Ellie shot Justin a fuming glance, especially as she saw that he looked just as fashionably elegant as he always did, with not a hair showing out of place beneath the tall hat he took off and handed to Stanhope once they had entered the grand entrance hall. 'I shall take

Chapter Fourteen

It was a belief that was instantly born out by Justin's next accusing comment. 'What are *you* doing here?'

Ellie flinched at the angry displeasure she could hear in his voice, knowing she would shrivel and die a little inside if he should ever speak to her in so disparaging a tone.

But the elegantly lovely woman standing across the hallway did not so much as blink in response to that harshness as she turned to smile at the discreetly departing Stanhope before answering Justin chidingly, 'Really, darling, is that any way to address me when we have not seen each other for so many months?'

'And whose fault is that?'

She smiled sadly. 'On this particular occasion I believe it to be your own.'

Ellie felt as if this entire day had turned into a nightmare she could not wake up from. Firstly, the fierceness of their lovemaking in Justin's carriage, which had once again ended so disastrously. And now, it appeared, she

She never had, Justin acknowledged begrudgingly, having always considered his mother to be one of the loveliest women he had ever set eyes upon. As a child he had thought her as beautiful as any angel. And she continued to be, despite now being in her late forties.

Her fashionably styled hair was as golden and abundant as it had ever been, her blue eyes as bright, her face and throat as creamily smooth, her figure still as resplendently curvaceous in the blue gown she wore—

The blue gown she wore…?

To Justin's knowledge his mother had not worn anything but black since the death of his father three years ago. And yet today, here and now, she was wearing a fashionable silk gown the same colour blue as her eyes, satin slippers of the same shade peeping out from beneath the hem of that gown.

Did this mean that his mother had finally—finally!—decided to end her years of solitary mourning for his father?

Ellie could only stare at the woman Justin had just introduced as his mother.

Was it any wonder she had assumed her to be something else entirely? This tall, beautiful woman definitely did not look old enough to be Justin's mother. Did not look old enough to be Ellie's own mother!

'I am sorry we did not meet when your mother and Frederick were alive, but so pleased that we are doing so now.' Rachel St Just smiled warmly as she seemed to glide across the hallway to where Ellie stood, the

mockery that were such a part of her son's nature, knowing herself to be neither 'beautiful' nor a 'paragon'—especially now, when her appearance was so bedraggled! But she could discern only kindness in the duchess's face as she continued to smile at her warmly.

Another glance at Justin showed that cynicism and mockery to be all too visible on *his* too handsome face! 'The dowager duchess is too kind,' Ellie answered his mother quietly.

'My mother-in-law is indeed kind,' Rachel agreed. 'But, I assure you, in this instance she was being truthful as well as kind.'

'Are you seriously telling me that you have decided to give up your years of solitary mourning in the country—' Justin eyed his mother derisively '—to come up to town out of a mere curiosity to meet Eleanor?'

The duchess raised golden brows. 'Why, what other reason can there have been?'

His jaw tightened. 'Grandmama did not write and tell you she has recently been...indisposed?'

Ellie saw now where Justin was going with this conversation. He was concerned that Edith might have confided more fully as to the seriousness, or otherwise, of her illness with her daughter-in-law than she had him, and it was that very confidence which was now the reason for his mother's unexpected, and for Justin obviously surprising, return to town.

'I believe I will leave the two of you now and go to my room to bathe,' Ellie spoke softly into the tenseness of the silence that had now befallen them all.

That brought her gaze swiftly back to him, those green eyes flashing her displeasure. 'That will not be necessary, your Grace, when I have every intention of going to bed and then to sleep shortly afterwards.'

And she was no doubt hoping—perhaps even praying?—that when she awoke, this afternoon would turn out to be nothing but a nightmare!

Justin's own life was also becoming increasingly unbearable. Not only did he still have his grandmother's illness to worry about, and now his mother's unexpected arrival at Royston House to ponder over, but Dryden Litchfield, and his possible connection to Eleanor, still lurked threateningly in the background of these other, more immediate, concerns.

Boredom? Hah! Once again Justin acknowledged that he no longer had the time in which to suffer that emotion!

'Very well.' He thrust a hand through his hair. 'But if your headache worsens I wish for you to ring for Stanhope immediately, so that Dr Franklyn can be sent for.'

'I am not a child, Justin, to be told by you what I should or should not do!' Eleanor's cheeks instantly coloured a vivid red as she remembered they had an interested audience listening to their conversation. Her tone had been scathing to say the least, her use of his first name implying a familiarity between them which had certainly not been apparent until now. 'I apologise, your Grace,' she made that apology pointedly to his mother rather than Justin—obviously implying she did not feel

which you feel the need to discuss with either Edith or myself, Justin?'

Justin continued to watch Eleanor for several more seconds as she hurriedly ascended the curved staircase, only turning his attention back to his mother once she had reached the top of those stairs and disappeared rapidly down the hallway he knew led to her bedchamber. 'Such as?' He eyed his mother coolly.

She sighed. 'I see that you are still angry with me.'

'Not at all.' His mouth twisted. 'Anger would imply a depth of emotion which simply does not exist between us.'

His mother gave a pained frown. 'That is simply not true! I have always loved you dearly, Justin—'

'Oh, please!'

'But—'

'I have no intention of continuing this conversation out here in the hallway, where anyone might overhear us.' He turned to stride in the direction of the Blue Salon, waiting until his mother, having hesitated briefly, now entered the room ahead of him, before following her and closing the door firmly behind her. 'Why are you really here, Mother?'

'I told you—'

'Some nonsense about meeting Eleanor.' Justin waved away his impatience with that explanation as he stood with his back towards one of the bay windows that looked out over the front of the house. 'To my knowledge, Eleanor has resided at Royston House

to hell with what deductions his mother might care to make in that regard.

Eyes so like his own dropped from meeting his as his mother instead ran a fingernail along the piping at the edge of the cushion upon which she sat. 'It is not so sudden, Justin. I have known for some time that one of us must attempt to heal the breach which exists between us. And when you failed to visit me on my birthday this week, I realised it must be me.'

Justin had completely forgotten that it *was* his mother's birthday just four days ago. Indeed, he had been so preoccupied, with both his grandmother's illness, and this unaccountable passion he had developed for Eleanor Rosewood, that he was no longer sure what day of the week it was, let alone that he had missed altogether his mother's forty-ninth birthday!

He winced. 'Once again I apologise.'

She gave a teasing tilt of her head. 'Enough to give me the kiss you failed to give me earlier?'

'Of course.' Justin crossed the room to briefly press his lips against the smoothness of her cheek; it was a small price to pay, after all, for such negligence.

His mother nodded. 'And will you now sit here beside me and tell me all about Miss Rosewood?' She patted the sofa cushion beside her own.

A gesture Justin ignored as he instead walked over to one of the armchairs placed either side of the unlit fireplace. He folded his long length down into it in a deliberately relaxed pose, his elbows resting on the arms of the chair as he steepled his fingers together in front

But those years, when he had very often not seen his mother or his father for months at a time, had created a gulf between them which he truly believed to be insurmountable.

'It is not my intention to be cruel to you, Mother. I just—why can you not just accept that there is too much between us, too many years spent apart, for us to be able to reach any common ground now?'

There was a strained look beside those tear-wet eyes and lines beside her unsmiling mouth. 'There are things—' she broke off, as if seeking the right words to say to him. 'You asked why I have come up to town. The truth is, when you forgot even to acknowledge my birthday, I decided—'

'Damn it, I have already apologised for my oversight!'

She shook her head. 'It is still a symptom of the way our relationship now stands. And there are things you should know, things I have not told you before now, which I think you have a right to know.'

Justin frowned. 'There is nothing you can say to me now that could ever take away all those years of neglect, when you chose to travel about the world with your husband—'

'My husband was your father, don't forget that! And we did not spend our lives simply enjoying ourselves, as you seem to be implying we were!' Her expression was anguished, her gloved hands clenched tightly together in her agitation. 'Nor was my decision to accompany him an easy one to make. But I made sure you were

'And he was.'

'Then I do not see—'

'That business was not his own!'

'Then whose was it?' Justin made no attempt to hide his growing impatience with this conversation.

She looked rather irritated now. 'Can you really not guess, Justin?'

He stared at her, a critical gaze that his mother continued to meet unflinchingly, unwaveringly, as if willing him to find the answer for himself.

Justin tensed suddenly as an answer presented itself, sitting forwards in his chair suddenly. 'Can it be—?' He paused, shaking his head slightly in denial. 'All those years—did my father work secretly as an agent for the crown?'

He knew the answer he had found was the correct one, as a look of relief now flooded his mother's beautiful face, making it radiant.

and then the departure of the St Justs to Lady Littleton's soirée. Several hours later, she still hadn't heard that carriage return.

She had assumed—wrongly, she now realised—that Justin, despite his reluctance to attend such social occasions, would have accompanied his newly arrived mother, and grandmother, to Lady Littleton's for the evening.

'Eleanor…?'

Her lids remained stubbornly closed, despite the fact that she could now discern the glow of candlelight through their delicate membranes. Justin had obviously moved closer to where she lay in bed.

'Damn it, are there not already enough women in this household who prefer to avoid my company this evening!' he muttered truculently.

It was that very truculence, a cross little-boy emotion, and so at odds with his usual arrogant self-confidence, that caused her lids to finally open, in spite of her previous decision to ignore him and hope that he would just go away.

'Ah ha!' Justin looked down at her triumphantly as he stood beside the bed, lit candle held aloft.

Ellie turned to lie on her back and rest up against the pillows, the sheet pulled up over her breasts as she looked up at Justin guardedly in the candlelight. She quickly realised he seemed to be leaning against the bed for support, his appearance also less than presentable; he had removed his jacket and neckcloth completely some time during the evening, several buttons of his

of satisfaction. 'You have the hang of saying my name now, I see.'

'Justin!' she repeated with considerable exasperation as she took a grasp of his arm and shook it, with no apparent result as he simply settled more comfortably on to the pillows. 'You must get up now and leave immediately!'

'Why must I?'

'Your mother and grandmother will be returning soon—'

'They will not be back for hours yet.' He raised a hand to cover a yawn. 'And it was dashed lonely downstairs in the library on my own, whereas it is warm and cosy up here with you.'

Ellie stilled at this unexpected admission from a gentleman who gave the clear impression that he had never needed anyone's company but his own. 'Why is it that you think your mother and the dowager are avoiding your company?'

'Do they need a reason?' He gave a shrug.

To Ellie's mind, yes, they most certainly did; Rachel St Just had been so emotional earlier at seeing her son again, after what seemed to have been a lengthy separation, and the dowager was prepared to forgive her grandson anything since he had returned to live at Royston House. 'Why did you not accompany them to Lady Littleton's?'

He prised one lid open to look up at her. 'I may be in the mood for company, Eleanor, but I am not so desperate I would resort to that particular torture!'

'Did you know you have the most beautiful hair I ever beheld...?' Justin reached out to take a long red strand between his thumb and fingers. 'So soft and silky to the touch and like living flame to gaze upon.' He allowed the silkiness of her hair to fall through his fingers.

'I do not think this the time or the place for you to remark upon the beauty of my hair.'

'When else should I remark upon it when it is normally kept confined or hidden away beneath your bonnet?'

'Not always...' A blush brightened her cheeks.

No, not always...for had Justin not wound these silken tresses about his partially naked body just hours earlier?

He moved up on one elbow the better to observe how smooth and creamy her skin now appeared against that living flame. 'I could not see you properly in the carriage this afternoon.' He smoothed his hand across the bare expanse of her shoulder now clearly visible to him. 'You are very beautiful, Eleanor. Your skin is so soft...'

She held herself stiffly, but even so could not hide the quiver caused by the touch of his caressing fingers. 'Unless you have forgotten, Justin, I, too, am currently avoiding your company...'

He gave a wicked smile. 'I have forgotten none of what took place between us this afternoon, Eleanor.'

The colour deepened in her cheeks. 'Nor, unfortunately, have I. Which is why—'

'Unfortunately?' Justin's fingers curled about her

intention of ever becoming his mistress or any other man's, 'bedevilled by desire', or otherwise!

She drew in a sharp breath. 'You will leave my bed-chamber right now, sir!'

'Can't,' he mumbled.

'What do you mean, you can't?' She continued to glower down at Justin as she stood beside the bed upon which he still lounged so elegantly, inwardly decrying the fact that he still managed to look so impossibly handsome, despite his less-than-pristine appearance. Or perhaps because of it…

Justin looked far more of a fallen angel in his current state of dishevelment, the gold of his overlong hair having fallen rakishly across his brow, with similar gold curls visible at the open throat of his shirt.

He cracked open that single eyelid once again as he answered her. 'I mean, dear Eleanor, that if my cock is incapable of rising to the occasion after I have gazed upon your delicious near-nakedness, then you may rest assured the rest of me is incapable of rising too!'

Ellie felt the embarrassed colour burning her cheeks. 'You are both behaving and talking outrageously! And likely you will seriously regret it come morning. Indeed, I believe you will wholeheartedly deserve the debilitating headache that will no doubt strike you down—Justin!' She gave a protesting hiss as he reached out to grasp her wrist before tugging determinedly, causing her to tumble back down on to the bed beside him. 'Stop this immediately.' She fought against the arm and leg

in the way his eyes had darkened and those grim lines had become etched beside his mouth. 'And would this woman, this mother, happen to be your own?'

He nodded. 'For years I have believed my mother and father to have been so engrossed in their love for each other, in their need to be exclusively with each other, that they had no room or love to spare in their lives for me, their only child,' he rasped. 'And now this evening my mother has told me—I can trust you not to discuss this with anyone else…?'

'Of course.' She bristled slightly at his need to ask.

He nodded distracted. 'This evening I have learnt what my mother and grandparents have always known, that my father was a hero and worked secretly for the crown for many years. That he risked his own life again and again. And latterly my mother chose to put herself in that same danger, when she insisted on travelling with him after I had gone away to boarding school. The two of them succeeded in collecting information which has saved many hundreds of lives over the years.'

And it was obvious, from the mixture of pain and pride Ellie now detected in Justin's voice, that he had not decided as yet how he felt about that…

Not surprising, really, when he had so obviously become the cynical man that he now was because for so many years he had held a quite different opinion about his parents.

It also confirmed Ellie's previous belief that this might also be the reason Justin had repeatedly declared he had no intention of being in love with his own wife,

er's revelations, and an overindulgence of brandy after not eating enough at dinner, to loosen his tongue in a way he would not otherwise have done and had now appeared to have cast doubts in Ellie's mind about her own father.

How much worse would those doubts be if she were ever to discover that both Justin and the Earl of Richmond, suspected Dryden Litchfield of being her real father, as a result of his having raped her mother!

Damn it, here he was, wallowing in self-pity—probably exacerbated by that overindulgence of brandy, the effects of which seemed to have dissipated entirely during the course of this current conversation—when the truth was his own father had been a hero of major proportions, his mother, too, when they had both decided to travel to places that were often highly dangerous.

What an idiot he had been. How utterly bloody selfish. Instead of getting blind drunk, what he should have done earlier this evening was get down on his knees and thank his mother for all that she and his father had sacrificed for their king and country.

His mother had been right, of course, in that he *had* forgotten those years before he went away to boarding school. Happy and contented years when Justin had his mother's almost undivided attention, interspersed with weeks or months when his father would return to them and the three of them would then do those things together.

Eleanor, on the other hand, had no memories whatsoever of any father, either in her childhood, or now.

Ellie now sat up against the headboard of the bed, her legs curled up beneath her. 'Justin, you would…share the information with me, if you were to learn anything of my father which might damage the dowager duchess in society?'

He turned to look at her sharply. 'And what of your own reputation?'

She shrugged. 'I came from obscurity and will quite happily return there, but I could not bear to think that I had caused the dowager, or indeed yourself or your mother, any social embarrassment before I did so.'

Justin's expression softened. 'And would you not regret or miss anyone or any part of that society on your own account?'

Having been reluctant at first, Ellie knew she would now miss many things. The warmth and kindness of Edith St Just, and now her daughter-in-law, for one. The friendship of Magdelena Matthews, which, never having had a close female friend before now, had become so very dear to Ellie these past few days. And lastly, she would miss Justin himself.

She had not spent all of her time earlier this evening in bathing and eating a light supper, but had found more than enough time in which to dwell on what she truly felt for Justin. To come to the realisation, that much as she might wish it otherwise, she was indeed in love with him to the extent that, if she ever *were* to be rejected from society, from *his* society, that she might, out of a need to be with the man she loved, even go so far as to

Chapter Sixteen

'Something must be done about Litchfield, Richmond!' Justin voiced that same sentiment the following afternoon, scowling across the distance that separated the two men as they sparred together at Jackson's Boxing Saloon.

'I agree—if only so that you no longer feel the need to try to beat me into the canvas!' Lord Bryan Anderson drawled ruefully after Justin had landed a particularly vicious jab to his jaw. Both men were stripped to the waist, the perspiration from their efforts obvious upon their sweat-slicked bodies.

Justin drew back. 'Damn it! I apologise, Richmond.' He straightened before bowing to the other man, as an indication that he considered their bout to be a draw and now over.

The Earl of Richmond eyed him curiously as they strolled across to where they had left their clothes earlier, his muscled physique appearing that of a much younger man, the hair on his chest reddish-gold rather

was of a more serious nature than he had previously allowed for.

His mother's revelations about his father seemed to have somehow stripped away all of his defences, to such a degree that he could no longer hide the truth, even from himself.

He had been so determined to maintain his lack of emotional involvement where women were concerned, that he had not fully understood until after he had returned to his own bedchamber the previous night, completely sober but unable to sleep, the difference she had already made in his life.

The main change had been that he had moved back into Royston House, after years of refusing to do so. He might have excused that move to Eleanor as the need for him to be close at hand if his grandmother should become ill again, but inwardly he had always acknowledged that it was really Eleanor, and the need he felt to protect *her,* most especially from men such as Litchfield, that had been his primary reason for returning home.

A need to protect her which had just resulted in a deeper, even more startling, realisation…

'It is curious, is it not,' Richmond continued slowly, 'considering Litchfield's licentiousness, and obvious disregard for whether a woman consents or not, that there are not more of his bastards roaming the English countryside.'

Justin shrugged. 'We do not know that there are not.'

an acquaintance, but that does not give you licence to question me about my relationship with Eleanor.' Especially when Justin was unsure himself, as yet, as to exactly how to proceed with her!

The two men's gazes clashed in a silent battle of wills, Richmond the one to finally back down as he sighed. 'I apologise if I have given offence, Royston.' He gave a stiff bow.

'Your apology is accepted.' Justin smiled. 'In fact, if it is not too short notice, then why not join us for dinner this evening at Royston House, and then you may see for yourself how ill-treated Eleanor is!' he teased.

'I would never accuse you, or any member of your family, of ill treatment towards anyone,' Richmond protested.

'I trust you will allow me to make Litchfield the exception, if it becomes necessary?' Justin drawled, cracking his knuckles meaningfully.

'Let us hope that it does not.' Richmond grimaced. 'I have heard tell that your mother has recently returned to town.'

'All the more reason for you to rescue me from yet another evening of dining in an all-female household!'

The earl gave a rueful smile. 'In that case, I believe I should very much enjoy dining with you and your family this evening, thank you.'

'It is settled then.' Justin, now fully dressed and ready to depart, nodded his satisfaction with the arrangement. 'As it happens, I am expecting another report on Litchfield to be delivered later today, which we

long and frequent absences, and what he had believed to be their almost obsessive love for each other that they would abandon their only child in order to be together.

Just as she now believed it was the reason he had decided that such a love in his own marriage was not for him.

Unfortunately, that understanding made absolutely no difference to how she felt about him.

It was no longer the girlish infatuation she had felt for his rakish good looks and arrogant self-confidence just a few short weeks ago, but a deep and abiding love that would surely cause her heart to break when she had to leave him. As she surely must. Loving him as passionately as she did, marriage to another man had become an impossibility for her. But she also had to accept that one day Justin had to marry, if only to provide his heir—and she could not remain at Royston House as witness to such a cold and calculated alliance.

Except he was not married as yet, or even betrothed.

'Can you possibly be referring to Lord Bryan Anderson?'

Justin had been surreptitiously watching Eleanor until that moment, as he admired the creamy swell of her breasts visible above the low neckline of the deep-emerald silk gown she wore, a perfect match in colour for her eyes and lending a deep richness to the red of her hair as she sat demurely in the armchair beside the unlit fireplace.

It took some effort on his part to turn his gaze away

her feet to move to Justin's side—surely this latest disclosure would prove too much, even for him, on top of all he had been told about his father the previous day? Indeed, the hand he placed briefly in front of his eyes, as he shook his head, would seem to indicate as much.

Until he lowered that hand to reveal a teasing grin. 'Perhaps it is not too late, Mama? After all, you are now both widowed.'

'Justin!' his mother gasped, the blush deepening in her cheeks.

His grin widened. 'You could do far worse than Richmond, Mama. Did you meet him at the Royston Ball, Eleanor? And if so, what is your opinion of the man?' He turned to her, that mischief gleaming in the warm blue depths of his eyes.

Ellie returned Justin's smile as she gratefully responded to the warmth in his eyes. 'I danced a quadrille with him, I believe, and found him to be a very charming and handsome gentleman.'

Justin quirked a mocking brow. 'Not too charming or handsome, it is to be hoped?'

Now it was Ellie's turn to blush. 'In a fatherly sort of way,' she finished quickly.

Justin continued to study her admiringly for several long seconds. They had not had the chance to talk alone together as yet today and he had felt slightly wary about trying to do so, uncertain of his welcome after his reprehensible behaviour the night before in such an inebriated state. But he had felt slightly reassured a few moments ago when she had come to stand beside him

She looked uncertain. 'I believe that must be the earl I hear arriving now,' she murmured.

Justin was not so sure as he heard the sound of a raised voice outside in the hallway, followed by Stanhope's quieter, more reasoning tone, and then another shout.

'Justin, can you see what that is all about?' The dowager looked concerned.

He nodded, releasing Eleanor's elbow. 'Stay here,' he advised the women before crossing the room in long determined strides. He had barely reached the door before it was flung open to reveal an obviously furious Dryden Litchfield standing on the other side of it and an uncharacteristically ruffled Stanhope just behind him.

Litchfield's face was mottled with temper as he glared at Justin contemptuously. 'Just who the hell do you think you are, Royston?' he snarled.

'There are ladies present, Litchfield,' Justin reminded with cold menace.

'I don't give a damn if there is royalty present!' The other man's voice rose angrily. 'You have a bloody nerve, poking and prying about in my private affairs—'

'I remind you once again that there are ladies present!' Justin held on to his own temper with difficulty, inwardly wishing to do nothing more than to punch Litchfield on his pugnacious jaw, an action as unacceptable, in front of the ladies, as was the other man's swearing.

Litchfield snorted. 'I am sure they are all well aware of what an interfering bastard you are—'

you do not do as I suggest, then I will have no choice but to have you arrested forthwith.'

'Arrested?' Litchfield scorned. 'For what, pray?'

'I believe there are any number of charges which might be brought against you.'

'By whom? You?' he sneered.

'If necessary, yes,' the earl bit out grimly.

Litchfield gave a contemptuous shake of his head. 'I believe all your years of being married to a madwoman must have addled your own brain, Richmond—' His words came to an abrupt halt as the earl's fist landed squarely on his jaw, his eyes rolling back in his head even as he toppled backwards.

Stanhope, in a position to catch him as he fell, instead stepped aside and allowed the other man to drop to the marble floor of the grand entrance hall, his top lip turned back contemptuously. 'Shall I have one of the footmen assist me in ridding us of this...person, your Grace?' He looked enquiringly at a grim-faced Justin.

'Yes—'

'No,' Richmond put in firmly before turning to bow to all the St Just family. 'I apologise for my impertinence.' He looked at the duke, his expression stern. 'But information has come into my keeping this evening which I believe dictates we must settle this matter with Litchfield once and for all right now, Royston.'

Ellie was still bewildered by Lord Litchfield's insulting remark about her mother. Shocked that this obnoxious man should have even known the sweet and gentle Muriel! Nor did she completely understand his

Chapter Seventeen

'You will ask chef to delay dinner for half an hour,' Rachel St Just instructed Stanhope once the butler and a footman had deposited Litchfield on the rug in front of the unlit fireplace, the dowager having refused to allow him to soil any of the Georgian furniture with his less-than-clean appearance. 'After which, you may come back and remove him from our presence,' she added with a disdainful curl of her top lip.

Justin had never admired his mother more than he did at that moment, the truths she had told him yesterday at last allowing him to see her for the redoubtable woman that she was, rather than the mother he had believed to have abandoned him for so many years.

Richmond, he noted abstractly, was also regarding her with similar admiration.

'Justin...?'

He drew his breath in sharply, knowing he had been avoiding looking at Eleanor for the past few minutes as he saw to the removal of Litchfield, knowing he

dearing combination of more tender emotions in him before now.

'You are keeping something from me,' she spoke with certainty as she refused to sit down.

He straightened tensely, a shutter falling over those deep-blue eyes. 'Eleanor—'

'Royston is not the one responsible for keeping something from you,' the Earl of Richmond interrupted firmly.

'Then who is?' she wanted to know.

'I am.' The earl looked uncharacteristically nervous as he crossed the room to take one of Ellie's hands in his both of his. 'And it is my sincerest wish—'

'What the hell are you doing, Richmond?' Justin exploded, immediately filled with a possessive fury that the handsome man was touching her so familiarly. He still wasn't sure Richmond didn't have a *tendre* for her.

'Justin, please...!' His mother sounded distraught at his aggression.

His glittering blue gaze remained fixed on Bryan Anderson, his jaw clenched. 'Take your hands off her!'

Ellie blanched. 'I do not believe Lord Anderson means to give offence, Justin,' she murmured.

'He is offending me by touching you!' Justin continued to glower at the older man. 'I told you to let her go!'

'Really, Justin, do try to remember the earl is a guest in our home,' his mother reproved. 'Your own invited guest, in fact.'

Lord Anderson gave Ellie's fingers a reassuring squeeze before releasing her to turn and bow to the two

there is no need, when you have already stated that Litchfield was not the one responsible?'

'He is not.' Richmond's face appeared very pale against his white shock of hair and black evening clothes. His gaze returned to Eleanor. 'May I first say how like your mother you are, my dear.'

She blinked. 'You knew my mother?'

He nodded. 'Many years ago, in India.'

Her throat moved as she swallowed before speaking. 'Then you must have known my father, too?'

'I was Henry Rosewood's commanding officer.' Richmond told her. 'He was a well-liked and heroic officer.'

A tinge of pleased colour warmed Eleanor's cheeks. 'I never knew him, and—my mother talked of him so rarely.'

'Perhaps because it was too painful for her to do so,' the earl suggested gruffly.

'Perhaps.' Eleanor smiled sadly.

'The likeness between you and your mother is—startling. I had no difficulty in instantly recognising you as Muriel's daughter when I first saw you the evening of the Royston Ball,' Richmond continued emotionally. 'A fact I noted to the duke shortly afterwards.'

'He did not mention you had done so.' Eleanor gave Justin a brief puzzled glance.

'Perhaps because I did not see it as being of particular importance at the time.' He shrugged.

'But it is now?'

Justin had admired Eleanor for her intelligence more

Ellie was none the wiser for this explanation. 'But surely this can have nothing to do with me?'

'I am afraid it has everything to do with you, my dear.' The dowager raised her hands in apology. 'But I had no idea, when I made my request to Justin, that the matter would become so complicated.'

Again, Ellie was no nearer to understanding this conversation than she had been a few minutes ago. 'And what request did you make of Just—the duke?'

'I merely—I had realised—' The dowager appeared uncharacteristically flustered as she quickly crossed the room to take both Ellie's hands in her own. 'There is no easy way to say this, my dear, so I shall simply state that Henry Rosewood was killed in battle exactly a year before you were born.'

Ellie literally felt all the colour drain from her cheeks as she absorbed the full import of this statement. Henry Rosewood could not have been her father.

She stumbled slightly as she pulled her hands free of the dowager's to drop down into the armchair she had earlier refused. Tears blurred her vision as she looked up at Justin accusingly. 'You knew about this.' It was a statement, not a question.

A nerve pulsed in his tightly clenched jaw. 'Yes.'

'How long have you known?'

'A week, no more. Eleanor—'

'No! Don't!' She lifted a restraining hand as Justin would have moved to her side, grateful when he halted in his tracks. She needed to—had to somehow try to assimilate exactly what this all meant to her.

pletely white. You see, my wife of only a few months was involved in a hunting accident, from which she never fully recovered, physically or mentally. We never had a true marriage again.'

'So you were married when you and my mother—when the two of you—'

'I was,' he confirmed grimly.

Darkness started to blur the edges of her vision as the shock of it all suddenly hit her with the force of a blow, that darkness growing bigger, becoming deeper, as she felt herself begin to slip away.

'Out of my way, Richmond!' she heard Justin shout, before strong arms encircled her just as the darkness completely engulfed her and she collapsed into unconsciousness.

'For goodness' sake, stop your infernal pacing, Justin, and go up to the girl if that is what you wish to do!'

Justin made no effort to cease his 'infernal pacing' as he shot his grandmother a narrow-eyed glare. 'I am the last person Eleanor wishes to see just now.'

'Nonsense!' the dowager dismissed briskly. 'Once she is over the shock she will be gratified to know she is the daughter of an earl—'

'The illegitimate daughter of an earl!'

'I am sure Richmond will wish to acknowledge her as his own.'

'Whether he does or he does not, I very much doubt that Eleanor will thank any of us for our part in this,' Justin muttered dully. 'In just a few short minutes

over like a protective hawk with its newly hatched chick by Bryan Anderson.

By her real father…who had a lot more authority to be there than Justin did.

The earl had spared only enough time, as they waited in Eleanor's bedchamber for the doctor to arrive, to tell them all briefly how it had come about.

Richmond's own enquiries into the events in India twenty years ago had resulted in more than just the damning information he had gathered on Dryden Litchfield. He had received a letter earlier this evening, from the wife of a fellow officer who had also been a particular friend of Muriel Rosewood, in which she had stated that Muriel had given birth to a baby girl exactly nine months after leaving India. Exactly nine months after Bryan Anderson had spent a single night with Muriel before she sailed back to England.

'Do not judge him too harshly, Justin,' his mother now advised as she placed her hand gently on his arm. 'He had already lived five years of hell with his deranged wife when this occurred. It is all too easy, during wars and hardship, for such things as this to occur. And let us not forget that Lord Anderson offered Muriel refuge in his own home following Litchfield's attack upon her.'

'Before then bedding her himself!'

'Eventually, yes,' she allowed. 'But you know him well enough to realise it would not have been without her consent. And, as a woman, I can tell you exactly why Muriel would have welcomed the attentions of a

grandmother. 'What other deep dark secrets are we to be made privy to now?'

The dowager pursed her lips. 'I am afraid I was not completely truthful with you last week regarding my own health, my boy.'

He rolled his eyes. 'It was all a ruse, was it not, Grandmama? Another effort on your part to persuade me into residing at Royston House once more? To eventually get used to the idea of matrimony?'

The dowager's eyes widened. 'You knew all the time?'

'I was certain that was the case, yes,' he allowed with a wry smile. 'You hadn't allowed anyone else to be present in the room, even Eleanor, during Dr Franklyn's visits. Nor am I so lacking in intelligence that I did not see the vast improvement in your health within hours of my having moved back here. Tell me, Grandmama, how did you achieve the effect of the whitened cheeks that night you sent for me?'

The dowager gave a sniff of satisfaction. 'A little extra face powder was most convincing, I thought.'

'Oh, most,' Justin conceded drily. 'No doubt your letters to my mother these past months, informing her of Eleanor's introduction into society, and my own presence back at Royston House, were also part of your machinations?'

'You are being impolite, Justin!' The dowager looked suitably affronted.

'But truthful?'

'Perhaps,' she allowed airily.

Chapter Eighteen

Ellie was quite unprepared for the way Justin burst into her bedchamber, only seconds after the doctor had departed.

'What do you mean by entering Ellie's bedchamber uninvited, Royston?' Richmond frowned his disapproval of the younger man's actions.

To say this past hour had been…life-changing for her would be to severely understate the matter. To learn that Henry Rosewood, a man she had never known, was not her father after all and that Lord Bryan Anderson, the Earl of Richmond, was, had come as a complete shock to her.

But once she had got used to the idea, it was actually a pleasant one.

She should perhaps continue to be shocked, distraught, and take weeks, if not months, to acclimatise herself to the things she had learnt this evening, to all that Lord Anderson had gently explained had befallen her poor mother in India twenty years ago.

'But a pleasant one.' She turned to reach up and clasp her father's hand, the earl returning the shyness of her smile with one of warm affection. 'Justin, may I present my father, Lord Bryan Anderson, the Earl of Richmond. Father, Justin St Just, the Duke of Royston.'

Justin's admiration for this young woman grew to chest-bursting proportions at the gracious elegance and ease with which she made the introductions. Most females in Eleanor's present situation would be having fits of hysterical vapours by now, crying and carrying on to an unpleasant degree. But she was made of much sterner stuff than that, had so obviously absorbed, and then swiftly accepted her change in circumstances.

'Richmond.' He nodded stiffly to the older man.

'Royston.' The earl's nod was just as terse.

Eleanor gave a puzzled smile. 'I thought the two of you were friends?'

'We were,' the two men said together.

She looked taken aback. 'What has happened to change that?'

Richmond gave a humourless smile. 'Will you tell her, Royston, or shall I?'

Justin's frustration was evident as he glared at the earl; this was not the way he had wanted to approach this. 'I am afraid, Eleanor, that your father seems to be aware of the closeness that exists between us and he is feeling protective and disapproving, to say the least.'

'Oh,' she gasped, her cheeks flushing a becoming rose.

'It would be impossible not to know,' Richmond

you, nothing has happened that the duke should ever feel he must propose marriage for.'

'If you would allow us a few minutes alone, Richmond?' Justin quirked a questioning brow at her father.

'My answer will not change—'

'Richmond?' Justin spoke ruthlessly over Ellie's objection.

'I believe, Eleanor, that it is in your own best interest to listen to what Royston wishes to say to you,' the earl encouraged, satisfied that Justin wanted to do the honourable thing by his daughter.

Her lips pressed stubbornly together. 'My answer will not change, no matter what he has to say. And Justi—his Grace is well aware of the reasons why it will not.'

'It is always a bad sign when she resorts to calling me that,' Justin confided, smiling ruefully.

Richmond did not return the smile. 'You understand that I will fully accept whatever decision Eleanor makes?'

He sobered. 'I do.'

'Very well,' the earl said briskly. 'I will rejoin the two ladies downstairs. I am sure I must still have some explaining to do in that quarter.' He grimaced.

Eleanor looked distraught. 'There is no need for you to leave—'

'There is every need, damn it!' Justin's temper was not as even as he wished and he made a visible effort to suppress it.

'I will not leave the house until I have spoken to you

my love, prove it to you, and perhaps one day persuade you into loving me in return?'

Ellie felt numb as she stared down at him, sure that this usually proud man could not just have declared on bended knee that he was in love with her and that he wished to make her his duchess.

'There will never be anyone else for me, Eleanor,' he continued fervently at her continued silence. 'Much as I did not want to ever fall in love with any woman, I know that I love you beyond life itself. I think I've been in love with you since the night of my grandmother's illness when you summoned me here—which was not a true illness, by the way, but a wilful machination on her part to persuade me into moving back here—and then you brought me to task for my tardiness.'

'The dowager was not really ill?' Ellie found it safer to focus on that part of his statement rather than those other wonderful—unbelievable!—things he was saying to her.

'Not in the least,' Justin said with a twinkle. 'Nor was it my true reason for moving back to Royston House.'

'What was your true reason?' Ellie's heart was now beating so loudly in her chest she felt sure he must be able to hear it. Justin had said that he loved her. More than anyone and anything. Beyond life itself!

'To protect you,' he revealed grimly. 'From Litchfield and other men like him.' He sighed deeply before admitting, 'Also I know now that I was beside myself with jealously of the attentions being shown to you by

into his arms and the two of them became lost in the wonder of their love for each other.

One floor below them, in the Blue Salon, Edith St Just smiled with a quiet inner satisfaction at the knowledge that, on the morrow, she would be able to show her two closest friends the name of the young lady, written on a piece of paper to be held in safekeeping by Lady Jocelyn's butler, in which she had predicted who would become Royston's duchess.

That name was Miss Eleanor Rosewood…

* * * * *

"I couldn't." Annorah hesitated, biting her lip.

"Then take it off, too." He pushed his trousers past his hips and kicked them off, leaving only his smalls—a concession to her modesty. He turned around and Annorah blushed, her gaze looking everywhere but at him.

"Don't tell me you're embarrassed by my natural state." Nick spread his arms wide from his sides and sauntered toward her. He couldn't resist having a bit of fun. If he'd learned one thing about her this afternoon, it was that she could be teased—the wildness inside was very much alive once she let down her guard. He rather enjoyed getting past that guard, as he had in the river.

"It's not that."

"It isn't? Then is it perhaps that you're embarrassed about your natural state? I think your natural state would be quite lovely." He reached a hand down to her and tugged, letting the teasing fade from his voice. "Come on, Annorah. It's just the two of us. You've been eyeing that swimming hole since we got here. You know you want to." *You want to do more than swim, and if you'd look at me, you'd know I do, too.*

He had her on her feet and then he had her in his arms, kissing her—her throat, her neck, her lips. She tasted like wine, her body all compliance beneath his mouth. A soft moan escaped her. His hands worked the simple fastenings of her gown. He hesitated before pushing the dress down her shoulders, giving her one last chance to back out. If she resisted now, he'd let her. But she didn't. He smiled to himself. Sometimes all a person needed was a nudge.

HHEXP1213R